the Best-Kept Secret

the
Best-Kept
Secret

Emily Rodda

Illustrated by Noela Young

AN AVON CAMELOT BOOK

First published by Angus & Robertson Publishers in Australia and in the United Kingdom in 1988.

AVON BOOKS
A division of
The Hearst Corporation
105 Madison Avenue
New York, New York 10016

Text copyright © 1988 by Emily Rodda
Text illustrations copyright © 1988 by Noela Young
Published by arrangement with Angus & Robertson Publishers, a division of Gordon & Gotch Ltd.
Library of Congress Catalog Card Number: 89-26842
ISBN: 0-380-75870-9
RL: 5.0

First Avon Camelot Printing: May 1991

CAMELOT TRADEMARK REG. U.S. PAT. OFF. AND IN OTHER COUNTRIES, MARCA REGISTRADA, HECHO EN U.S.A.

Printed in the U.S.A.

OPM 10 9 8 7 6 5 4 3 2 1

For my dear friends at A&R.
with love

Contents

1

Windy Day on Marley Street

Joanna walked home, down Marley Street, and the leaves skidded past her, scratching on the footpath.

It was Friday, and her schoolbag was heavy with folders and library books, but the wind at her back pushed her along, so she didn't really notice. She walked quickly, thinking, looking at the leaves.

"Jo! Wait!" Cecilia came puffing up behind her. "Didn't you hear me? Why didn't you wait for me? I was right at the back of the bus, and by the time I got off you were . . ."

"Sorry, I didn't hear. I was thinking." Jo stopped and looked at Cecilia blankly, her close-cropped black hair standing up spiky in the wind.

Cecilia stood stolidly in the leaves, hands on hips. She shook her head and opened her blue eyes wide. "You're turning into an absent-minded professor, Jo," she warned, only half joking. "You'd better watch it."

"Ha, ha!"

They walked on in silence, past the magazine shop, the dry cleaner's, the pharmacy, the shoe-

repair shop with its black-and-gold sign, W. BREAN—
QUALITY SHOE REPAIRS. Across the road some younger
children played on the vacant block of land next to
the community center. Excited by the wild weather,
they screamed and ran around madly like puppies
let out for exercise, pretending to jump against the
wind, falling hysterically and rolling around in the
fallen leaves. Their shouts bounced against the shop
fronts opposite, echoing across the road and making
people turn and look.

"Idiot kids!" Mr. Brean's scowling face popped out
of his door like a cranky puppet's. He nodded his
bald head violently and spoke directly to Jo and Cecilia, as if they were somehow to blame for the noise.
"I dunno what they teach you kids at school!" He
gestured across the road angrily. "Get away! Get on
home, the lot of you!"

Jo and Cecilia hurried on. Cecilia giggled, and
sneaked a look over her shoulder. "He's weird," she
muttered.

"I wonder why he's so cranky. He can't always
have been like that," said Jo, trying to imagine Mr.
Brean as a younger man, without all those crabby
lines on his face, Mr. Brean working away mending
shoes, when the shop was new, the workbench
smooth and unmarked and the sign freshly painted.
"I wonder what made him . . ."

"Oh, who cares!" said Cecilia impatiently. "He's
just weird."

Jo shrugged. Cecilia had it all worked out. She'd
been like that ever since Jo met her in kindergarten,
when she'd had blond bangs and short, fair braids,
a plump, placid little face, and a neat pink suitcase
with Holly Hobbie on it. Even then she'd been able
to sum up the world and its people without any trou-

ble. People, to Cecilia, were "nice"—that is, like Cecilia and her family—or they were "weird." It made life very uncomplicated. Jo had always wished that she could be as sure of herself as Cecilia was.

Cecilia's elbow dug into her side. "Don't look! There's The Shark!" she hissed through clenched teeth. "Don't look!"

Heads down, smothering nervous giggles, they clung together and hurried past the fish-and-chips shop where Shark Murphy, carroty hair bristling in the wind, slouched against the green-tiled wall. His eyes were pale in his freckled face, and he ate hot french fries with black-stained fingers.

They were nearly past him when Cecilia, shoulders shaking, cheeks pink and flushed, gave a giggling snort. The Shark turned his head to look, and his eyes narrowed. With a little shriek Cecilia pulled away from Jo, took to her heels, and went pounding down the street, fair curls bouncing. The Shark looked after her and then turned cold eyes on Jo. She stared back at him fascinated, feeling like a little bird hypnotized by a snake.

She felt her heart pounding and her throat tighten. The Shark was a bad one—everyone said so. He'd dropped out of school; he'd been caught robbing phone boxes, and then stealing cars. He'd been to jail—or at least to a boys' detention center. His parents had given him up, people said, and moved away. Now he just hung around the streets doing odd jobs at the garage, tinkering with the old car that always stood outside the boardinghouse where he lived. He never smiled. He rarely spoke. He always looked dirty. He was scary.

Jo tore her eyes away from his and backed away. She turned and walked quickly on down the street, not looking back. Every moment she expected him to call out to her. She expected to hear his heavy steps behind her or even see his tattooed arm come down in front of her to bar her way. But nothing happened, and after a minute she glanced behind her. The Shark hadn't moved from his place by the wall. He was eating fries slowly, staring into space.

2

What's Happening?

Feeling a bit silly, Jo hurried on, her schoolbag bumping against her leg. Cecilia was nowhere to be seen. Jo passed Mr. Angelo's fruit stand, the health-food store, and the hairdresser's and with relief crossed Lily Street. She waved to old Simon Crisp looking out, lonely, from his window, and ran the last few steps next door to her own front gate. It shut behind her with the familiar reassuring clang, and she ran past gray feathers of lavender up to the front door, kicking crinkled leaves, blown in from the street, out of the way. She was home, and it was Friday. Her heart lifted as she rang the door-bell and heard Podge the dog's excited barking begin. She touched the waving leaves of the potted plant that stood by the door. It was called Fred, and had always been there, ever since she could remember. She used to eat bits of it, as a baby, she was told, whenever she had the chance. "Poor Fred was in tatters by the time you were two," Simon next door always said. But Fred looked fine now. No doubt he was grateful to have survived her babyhood.

Her father answered the door with Podge snorting and dancing at his heels as a fresh gust of wind swirled leaves around Jo's feet.

"Hello, darling. Good day? Look out—in, in, we've just vacuumed the hall!" He shut out the wind and the invading, clattering leaves, holding the bounding Podge back with one foot.

Jo bent to pat Podge's soft spaniel ears. Now that the little dog was quiet, she could hear voices in the kitchen. She raised her eyebrows at her father.

"It's another agent, about the house," he said casually, watching her.

Jo's lips tightened, and she said nothing. She wandered after him down the hall.

An eager-looking young man in a suit was sitting at the kitchen table with Jo's mother. He got to his feet as they entered the room and smiled and nodded at Jo.

"I think we've finished now, Michael, so I'll get going," he said cheerfully. "I'll give you or your good lady a ring in the next few days, and give you a progress report." He bent over and smiled at Jo. His breath smelled of peppermint. "Looking forward to getting a nice new room and a bigger garden, I'll bet," he said. Jo smiled politely. Her smile felt very false. It probably looked false too, because the agent's own smile faltered a little. He turned rather abruptly and shook hands with Jo's mother. "See you soon, Helen," he said.

Michael went out with the agent, and Jo was left with her mother in the kitchen. Helen, slender and gentle, sipped tea and smiled. But Jo didn't say any-

7

thing. She just poured herself some milk and stood by the window, drinking it. The tiny paved courtyard behind the house was dappled with sunlight, and the shadows of the trees crisscrossed the pools of light.

"Jo, don't be sad," said Helen's soft voice behind her. She felt a light hand on her shoulder, but didn't turn around.

"We love this house too, you know, Jo. We've lived here since before you were born. But, darling, it's just too small for us now. It's not as if we're looking for a place outside this area, or anything. We'll still see plenty of Simon, if that's what you're worrying about. He won't be right next door anymore, sure. But he'll be over to see us all the time—really he will."

Jo bit at the rim of her glass. "It's not too small," she said through closed teeth. "We fit well."

"There are only two bedrooms. The yard's tiny. Jo, we've been through all this!" Underneath Helen's softly cajoling tone Jo could hear a thread of irritation beginning to twist. Well, she knew she was being irritating, but she couldn't help it. She didn't need this just now. She didn't want it. Home was one thing that had never changed. That was important. But she couldn't explain it, somehow. She went on biting at her glass.

Helen sighed and went over to the table. She picked up the sheet of paper the agent had left and then suddenly turned around with a little exclamation.

"Oh! Oh, I feel as though I've done this before. Or seen myself doing it before, or something. Déjà vu! How strange. Maybe I dreamt it. *Did* I dream it? I can clearly remember stepping up to the table, with you standing by the window, and picking up that . . ."

"Day what?" Interested in spite of herself, Jo turned to look at her mother.

"Déjà vu. Day-ja-voo. It's French. It means 'seen already,' or something like that. That feeling you get sometimes: 'I've done this before.' It happens to lots of people."

"I've never had that feeling," said Jo curiously.

"Haven't you? Maybe you're too young." Helen shook her head and looked at the paper in her hand. "It's weird."

Weird. Cecilia would think it was weird, for sure. Cecilia would think that she, Jo, was weird too, not wanting to move to a new house. Weird and babyish, wanting to cling on to a life she knew and was sure of, like a fluffy toy. Weird to think that moving away from this house was some sort of step out of the safe circle of childhood, already shrinking too fast for comfort. All those familiar places gone—all those little routines changed. . . . And Jo fought down another thought as she stared out into the little back courtyard where a single sparrow now hopped, feathers fluffing indignantly with every gust of wind. She had a feeling there was something her mother wasn't telling her. Some other reason for this sudden decision to move house. What was it?

Lots of times they'd walked, on Sunday afternoons, down Singer Street, or Telford Avenue, or one of the other tree-lined roads that ran off Marley Street, and she'd absently listened to Michael and Helen pointing out this house or that. But the conversation always ended the same way. Their own house was nice too, and it was comfortable, and big enough really. One day they'd move. Definitely. But not just now.

Then Michael would laugh and Helen would sigh, and that would be that.

But suddenly there were real-estate agents in the house. Suddenly a move seemed possible—even probable. Why?

Jo lay in bed and listened to the wind. It swept around the little house as though it was getting ready to gather it up and spin it away, like a house caught in a tornado in a cartoon. She could hear her mother and father talking softly in the kitchen. She lay with her eyes open until they started stinging, and the wind still blew. She heard someone tiptoe to her door. Mum. She closed her eyes and began to breathe evenly, as if she were asleep.

She heard Helen come in, felt her tuck the covers
around her. Helen stood for a moment beside the
bed, her hand on Jo's hair. Jo felt herself relax. The
extra warmth of the tucked-in blankets was stealing
luxuriously around her legs and shoulders. The
sound of the wind seemed farther and farther away
with every breath she took. Her thoughts grew fuzzy
and slow. She barely heard Helen tiptoe from the
room, and somehow she didn't feel like opening her
eyes again. She slept.

It was much later when Jo awoke. She lay very
still, and wondered. What was happening? What had
woken her?

And then she noticed the silence. The curtains
were open, and the full moon shone through her

windows, straight onto her face. And it was quiet. Very quiet. The wind had stopped.

She slipped out of bed and looked out. The moon lit up the courtyard, the fence, the buildings behind the house. And everything was dead still, as though she was looking at a painted scene. Not a leaf or a twig moved. And yet there was a nervous, thrilling feeling in the air. It was as though everything was tense, waiting, holding its breath. Jo felt a little flutter beginning in her stomach. And then, far away, she heard the town-hall clock begin to chime. She counted the strokes. It was midnight.

The last note had barely died away when the first dog began to bark. A rather timid little bark it was, to begin with. But then another dog joined in, and another, and soon it seemed as if all the dogs in the neighborhood, from fat little Podge in the kitchen to the mighty Great Dane on Singer Street, were barking in chorus. And as Jo watched, the scene outside came to life once more. A lizard scuttled across the paving stones, branches moved gently, a few leaves fell. Across the back lane windows were thrown open as people rudely awakened from cozy sleep yelled at the dogs.

Jo turned from the window, pulled the curtains closed, and got back into bed. She turned on her side and listened as one by one the dogs lost interest and dropped out of the chorus. She imagined them yawning, putting black noses onto paws and curling themselves up on their beds. She imagined their doggy minds, still vaguely puzzled by what had happened, but preferring, after a while, to think about more easily understood things—like food, warm blankets, and sleep.

Jo sighed and shut her eyes. And just as she felt

12

her thoughts starting to drift into dreams, just at that moment between waking and sleeping, too late to turn back, she heard, or thought she heard, far away up Marley Street, the sound of music.

3

The Vacant Block

"I'll say I heard the dogs!" said Michael, raising his voice slightly to combat the radio, when Jo asked him next morning. "And this cornflake-eating apology for a dog was the worst of the lot." Podge turned around from her breakfast to regard him with embarrassed eyes, one ear trailing foolishly in her cornflakes and milk.

Joanna felt restless. She got up from the breakfast table and began wandering around the room. Something was niggling at the back of her mind. She kept feeling that there was something she was supposed to do. Something . . .

"Jo, stop prowling! And turn off that radio, will you? It's driving me crazy."

Jo snapped off the switch as she passed, and in the sudden silence that followed, three things happened in quick succession. Podge lifted her head once more and, not even bothering to lick the dripping mustache of milk from her furry lips, growled warningly—Jo, Helen, and Michael cocked their heads, turned to one another, and said in chorus, "I can hear music!"—and the doorbell rang.

Cecilia jumped and jiggled impatiently on the doorstep. Jo could hear the music clearly now that she was outside. It was coming from farther up Marley Street—a piping, waltzing melody, strange and inviting.

"D'you want to go uptown with me, Jo? Can you hear? Quick, I want to see what's going on!"

Helen pattered up the hall in bare feet, with Podge in close pursuit. "What is it?" she said and, paying no attention to the fact that she was still in her dressing gown, went down the front path and leaned over the gate.

Jo saw Cecilia's eyes flick up and down Helen's tousled, skinny little figure wrapped in the old Chinese kimono, black hair tangling uncombed onto her shoulders. Jo felt a bit uncomfortable. Cecilia's mother was always dressed by nine in the morning. Her dressing gown was a neat, quilted affair that covered her from neck to ankle.

"Mum!" she whispered urgently.

"What?" Helen turned back from the street. And she looked so funny, hanging bare-legged on the gate, with Podge clawing desperately at her heels, that Jo smiled in spite of herself and forgot to feel embarrassed.

"I'm going uptown with Cecilia to see what it is. Okay?" she said.

"Okay," said Helen, jumping off the gate and holding Podge back by the collar as they slipped through. "I'd like to know what it is myself. It's very loud. It must be some sort of advertising thing. Maybe they're giving ice cream away or some-

15

thing. . . . Oh—hello, Simon. How's the bronchitis? You shouldn't be out in the wind."

"Good morning, Helen, Yody-Jo!" Simon Crisp's bald head with its fluff of light-brown hair nodded at them from the next-door gate. His gold-rimmed glasses flashed in the morning sun. "I'm not too bad today, Helen," he wheezed. "It's on the mend, I'd say."

Jo looked at him in concern. He didn't sound too well to her.

"Come on," whispered Cecilia, tugging at Jo's arm.

Jo waved to her mother and let Cecilia pull her up as far as Simon Crisp's gate. She paused for a moment.

"We're going uptown, Simon. Do you want any milk?"

"Not today, thank you, Yo. I have plenty. But I tell you what—I wish I could go myself. See what's going on up there. . . ." He coughed and gazed wistfully up Marley Street, holding on to the bars of the gate as though he were in jail.

"Stuck at home!" he grumbled. "Five days at the office I've missed already too."

"But that gives you time to do more inventing, doesn't it, Simon?" said Jo coaxingly. "You always say that the nights and weekends aren't enough, and you need more time if you're going to invent something that's really—"

"More time, more money, more space, more everything," wheezed Simon Crisp, shrugging. He bent over the gate and lowered his voice. "Actually, Yo, I have been doing a bit of work. Polishing up a few things—and making a little something for you. For your collection of Simon Crisp originals." He smiled

16

faintly. "But now I hear Mrs. Pickering upstairs has
been to the landlord—about the noise, you know.
And last week I must say the smell of that rubber
substitute wasn't so good—that experiment didn't
quite work out as I'd hoped. I can't think why . . ."
His voice trailed off, and he thought for a moment.
Then he shrugged. "I can't think why. But anyway, she complained about that, too." He shook his
head. "Looks like there might be a bit of trouble this
time, Yo."

Jo stared at him in dismay.

"Her name is Jo, not Yo, you know," said Cecilia
patiently, as though she were talking to someone
not quite right in the head.

Simon Crisp looked at her tolerantly. "Ah—yes—

17

it's a nickname, Yo is, dear. Joanna and I are very old friends. 'Yo' was her own baby name for herself. Before she could say 'Jo' properly, you see. I got into the habit of calling her that too. A bad habit, now that she's a young lady, I suppose."

"It's not. I like it," said Jo loyally, ignoring Cecilia's teasing smile.

The strange music rose in the distance, and Simon, Jo, and Cecilia glanced quickly up the hill toward the sound.

"Ah!" said Simon. "You'd better go. You'd better not miss out on . . . whatever it is. Go on! I'll be here when you get back. Can't get rid of me that easily."

He smiled and waved them on, and kept smiling as they walked quickly away up Marley Street. Jo turned and waved once, at the Lily Street corner, as he'd known she would. He waved back, and Jo went on across the road. Simon Crisp's arm dropped to his side. Slowly the smile faded from his face, leaving it sad and tired. His shoulders sagged. He stood on at his gate, holding the bars in his hands, and listened to the music.

They started running. Up the hill, past the fish-and-chips shop, kicking up the leaves lying in piles on the pavement, holding hands as the music grew louder and louder, past Mr. Brean's shoe-repair shop, and . . . there it was!

Across the road, where yesterday children had screamed and played, the vacant block was vacant no longer.

Brass poles glittered in the sun; painted horses reared with red, neighing mouths, bold eyes, and gleaming saddles; and the music played—piping, beckoning music, in waltz time.

18

Jo and Cecilia crossed the road with a crowd. Early as it was, Marley Street was milling with people, curious and chattering. How had this happened? Yesterday a vacant block of land; today a full-size carousel, surrounded by a neat red-and-white painted fence, with a tent guarding its entrance. It was amazing. It was wonderful. The crowd spilled across the grass.

4

Riders Walk In

Close up the merry-go-round was a bewildering, a magnificent, sight. It was the biggest Jo had ever seen, and the brightest. The horses were huge, and from their shiny hooves to the tips of their ears they gleamed. Their heads seemed to toss impatiently to the music as Jo looked, and their painted eyes seemed to scan the crowd boldly, as if they were looking for riders.

Jo's heart began to beat fast. She tugged Cecilia's hand.

"Let's have a go," she whispered.

"Merry-go-rounds are for little kids," said Cecilia flatly. "I haven't been on one since I was in kindergarten."

"This one's not for little kids. It's . . . Look at it! It's a really good one." Jo dragged the unwilling Cecilia closer. She leaned over the little fence and peered up at the shining mirrors, the fantastic painted scenes that decorated the center of the merry-go-round.

"Come on, Jo. This is boring. What are you staring at?" Cecilia was growing impatient.

"Cecilia, how did it *get* here?"

Cecilia shrugged. "A truck brought it last night, I suppose," she said. "Who cares? Look, there's The Shark!"

But Jo wasn't interested in The Shark today. Shaking off Cecilia's restraining hand and feeling for the money in her pocket, she began to make her way along the fence to the small striped tent marked TICKETS: RIDERS WALK IN.

"Jo!"

The tent flap was closed. People milled around the entrance, but no one was going in. It was as if they were all waiting for a signal. Jo hesitated, fingering her coins. Perhaps it wasn't open yet. But the music played, calling to her, and the sign said RIDERS WALK IN. Still she hesitated.

"Jo!"

Cecilia appeared at her shoulder and looked at her crossly, hands on hips.

"What's the matter with you? You're acting weird."

"It's interesting," said Jo stubbornly. "I'm going in. Are you coming or not?"

Cecilia sighed resignedly. "Oh, all *right.* What's the big deal, anyway?" She pushed casually at the tent flap, but it didn't move. She clicked her tongue and tried again. And again. She tugged at the tent flap with all her strength, but it remained tightly closed. She looked at her hand in comical surprise.

Jo felt her heart leap. *This* wasn't something that could be explained away. Oh, if only Simon had been able to come. He loved mysteries. He would have loved this! She glanced quickly around. Some people were watching closely. Perhaps they had tried to get in too and had failed.

"There, it's shut," hissed Cecilia, rather pink in the cheeks, for she too had noticed people watching them, and she hated being caught in a mistake. "This is stupid. Let's go."

But Jo shook her head. She was watching as someone else slouched toward the tent. Someone who pushed his way through the crowd, unsmiling, till he stood beside them at the entrance. It was The Shark.

The Shark looked at the notice. TICKETS: RIDERS WALK IN. The music played. The crowd watched. The Shark took hold of the tent flap, just as Cecilia had done. It moved under his fingers, and before they could blink, he had pushed it aside and disappeared into the green shadow within.

"But . . ." Cecilia almost stamped her foot. "How did he *do* that?"

Jo didn't answer. She had noticed Mrs. Pickering, Simon's complaining neighbor, who worked in the pharmacy, moving quietly up to the tent. Mrs. Pickering, cool, collected, gave the flap a firm tug. It gave not a ripple. Mrs. Pickering pulled away her hand as if it were burned and backed away. Then she turned and made off through the crowd, looking neither right nor left.

"Look," hissed Cecilia, "it's stupid, standing here gawking. It's some kind of trick. Some phony trick. They got The Shark to go in with them, to get everyone wanting a ride. Let's go!"

"Just a minute, Cecilia. Just hold on a minute."

Mr. Angelo from the fruit-and-vegetable shop stepped out of the crowd, smiling nervously, and

walked toward the tent. Despite his smile, his brow was wrinkled. He always looked tired and worried these days. Everyone noticed it. Jo's mother said she was sorry for him. He worked very hard, keeping his shop open from early morning to late at night without anyone to help him except a man who came in at the very busiest times. It was very unusual to see him away from the shop—especially on a Saturday morning.

A year ago he'd brought his mother from Italy. Back home she'd been all alone, and he'd saved up to bring her to join him. But she wasn't happy. Anyone could see that. She sat day after day in a corner of his shop, dressed all in black, never smiling, speaking only to him in an undertone.

"She misses her friends. She hates it here. I made a bad mistake," a miserable Mr. Angelo told Jo's mother one day. "She wanted to come. She begged me to save money fast so we could be together. But now she's sorry. I'm sorry. Every night she cries. She's an old lady. And there's no money to send her back. Not unless I sell the shop, anyhow." He'd sighed. "Maybe I should. I wonder what I'm working like this for, sometimes. Don't seem to be getting anywhere."

"Phil, she'll find her feet," Helen had said earnestly. "Like you say, she's an old lady. It's hard to get used to a different country, and people, and language, and everything. She'll settle down. She'll learn a bit of English, and then . . ."

But Mr. Angelo had given the smallest of smiles and shaken his head. "Maybe," he'd said. "Maybe." And he'd finished adding up the bill without another word.

Now Phil Angelo stood by the tent flap, looking at

24

the notice as if he didn't quite understand what he was doing there. He stretched out his hand, pulled back the canvas, and disappeared inside.

"Look at that!" "Let's see." "Excuse me, can I get through, please?" "Excuse me!" People pressed forward toward the tent. One by one they tried to get in. Mostly they failed. Pull and tug as they might, they had no more success than Cecilia and Mrs. Pickering had had, and they were forced to stand back and let others try their luck.

But then, every so often, someone would touch the tent flap, flick it aside, and slip through the opening without the slightest fuss. People would crane to see, the next person in line would pull at the canvas eagerly . . . but almost always the flap would be shut tight against them, and nothing they could do would move it.

Jo knew she had to try. She moved closer. Cecilia, infuriated by the whole thing, tugged at her arm.

"You don't want to go in there anyway, Jo. Come on! Let's go and buy a doughnut. Let's go and—"

But Jo's turn had come. She stepped forward eagerly, trying to shake off Cecilia's restraining hand.

"Cecilia, *don't!*"

"Jo . . ."

The tent flap moved under her hand. She pulled it aside.

"Jo!"

And in a flash she was inside. She was inside, and with her, holding tightly to her wrist, was Cecilia, very red and cross.

5

"The Time of Your Life"

"Yes, now, hello, hello!" Standing at one end of the tent was an old man, ushering people through a turnstile and up a ramp that obviously led to the carousel. He was small, weather-beaten brown, bald, and bent, and a gold earring flashed in one ear. He wore a pink shirt with silver bands around the elbows to keep his cuffs pulled up, and tight blue trousers with suspenders. He nodded and grinned at Jo, showing crooked white teeth, and patted the turnstile invitingly.

"Get your tickets!" he cackled. "Tickets for the time of your life. Ha!" He turned to some people waiting beside him and took their tickets. "Thank you, madam. Thank you, sir. Thank you, sonny. Read the notice? Understand the conditions? Good, then, off you go. This way, madam. Mind the step! Tickets! Tickets from the lady there, please. Hurry, hurry!"

The inside of the tent smelled of warm canvas and trodden grass. People milled uncertainly around. Jo caught a glimpse of Mr. Angelo over by the turn-

26

stile. He was holding a ticket, waiting to get through. The old man's voice cut through the warm air again. "No time to lose, ladies and gentlemen. Ha! Get your tickets." And Jo, with a wide-eyed Cecilia still in tow, crossed quickly to the rainbow-striped ticket booth.

Behind the counter was a sharp-faced old woman with fine, arched eyebrows. A thin, patterned scarf, intricately knotted and folded, covered her hair. She looked hard at Jo, and her thin lips curved in a knowing smile, but she said nothing.

"Ah . . . how much, please?"

"How much do you have, mademoiselle?" said the old woman calmly. Her hands, little and brown like monkeys' paws, the fingers covered with rings, tapped slowly on the counter.

"Well . . ."

"Jo," hissed Cecilia. "Let's get out of here!"

The old woman leaned across the counter, narrowed her eyes and peered at Cecilia.

"What is this? Ah, I see. An unexpected guest." She tapped her fingernails on the counter's edge. "I am afraid we cannot accommodate you, mademoiselle. You are not authorized."

Cecilia blushed and tightened her grip on Jo's arm. "How can you be authorized to ride a babies' merry-go-round?" she said defiantly.

The woman ignored her and fixed her eyes on Jo. "A coin, if you please," she ordered. "Any coin will do."

Jo fumbled in her pocket, pulled out some money, and laid it on the counter.

The woman nodded and slid a pink ticket into her hand.

"I . . . I want my friend to come too," said Jo ner-

vously, ignoring Cecilia's impatient whispering in her ear.

"There would be no point, *ma petite*," said the old woman without interest. "She has no place here. She is not a rider. That is obvious at first glance."

"She came in with me," said Jo insistently, not understanding a word of this, only knowing that she didn't want to go onto that carousel by herself. "Please." She pulled out another coin and pushed it into the woman's hand.

The woman looked at her, that half smile again curving her narrow lips. Suddenly she made up her mind and pushed another ticket across the counter.

"Very well," she said. "A wasteful exercise, but as it happens, we have a spare seat. Someone has not arrived, and we cannot wait. We are late begin-

28

ning as it is. It is not, after all, as if it has never happened before. I fear she will not be particularly good company, but you must have your way, mademoiselle. Now . . ." She became brisk and businesslike. "Please sign the book, and be quick! We must be off."

She pushed a large open book in front of Jo's nose, and tapped the page with a thin brown finger.

Jo picked up a pen lying on the counter. What was all this? She hesitated.

"*Tiens!*" exclaimed the old woman impatiently. "Why do you wait? We must go. Surely it is not that you have not yet read the sign?"

Jo stared at her, feeling stupid.

The old woman clicked her tongue, said something in what Jo took to be French, and let herself out of the booth with an annoyed thump. She appeared next to Jo and took her arm. She was tiny—only about as tall as Jo—but her grip was very strong. She steered Jo over toward a large sign near the tent entrance. "Read, please!" she ordered.

Jo read:

Important Notice. By Order.
Intending Riders Please Note.

The following conditions must be read and understood by all intending riders of this carousel (license no. 143).

1. This carousel is licensed to carry 46 riders and 3 carousel personnel only. Loads in excess of this limit are dangerous and strictly prohibited.

2. Alcohol, smoking, and the carrying of pets prohibited.

3. All care will be taken, but no responsibility will be accepted by the proprietors for any loss of property, emotional or physical hardship, or any other accident occurring to riders on this carousel.

4. According to bylaw no. 5a (i), this carousel may not exceed its prescribed time limit of seven years into future time under any circumstances.

5. Before ascending the carousel, all riders must sign the book provided, indicating their acceptance of the above conditions.

Jo stared wide eyed at the notice and shook her head. *"Seven years into future time"*?

She tried to make herself read the smaller print at the bottom of the notice, but her eyes wouldn't focus, and the fine print blurred.

"You have changed your mind, perhaps?" The old woman raised her eyebrows and held out her hand. "Return the tickets, then."

"Seven years into future time"!

"No, no, I want to go." Jo clutched the scraps of pink paper tightly against her chest.

The old woman shook her head and gave a low, chuckling laugh.

"Ah, it is always the same. You are afraid, is that not so? But you must go. You must." She laughed again. "Ah, you people are funny."

"We're not funny!" cried Cecilia, finding her tongue. "We think you're funny. And we don't believe in all this silly stuff either, do we, Jo? We know it's just a trick to get people in and get their money."

The old woman stared at her with half-closed eyes. "Be careful, mademoiselle. I have met your sort before." Between the heavy eyelids her dark eyes glittered with anger.

Cecilia backed away, feeling for Jo's hand.

"Please sign the book!" snapped the old woman, and thrust them toward the booth where the book lay open, waiting.

Jo picked up the pen. The book was big, bulky, and old, very old. Her eye ran over the list of names on the thick cream paper. She knew some of them—Mr. Angelo, Ettie Chase, a girl from school, old Mrs. Beattie from the nursing home. But there were lots of others. All the people she'd seen come into the tent had signed, it seemed. Right at the top there was a careless scrawl. Charles Murphy. The Shark. She'd never thought about his having a real name before.

There were two blank spaces at the bottom of the right-hand page. For her and Cecilia. But Cecilia hadn't been expected. She was taking someone else's place. Someone who, for some reason, hadn't arrived. And suddenly Jo knew who that someone was. Someone who would have given anything for this chance. Someone who was stuck at home nursing a miserable cough and an aching chest, listening to the carousel's call but unable to answer it. She thought furiously, but there was nothing to be done. Simon had been cheated of his chance.

She heard the old man's voice shouting at them impatiently, and the woman's answering call. The carousel music grew louder and faster, filling the tent with sound. An urgent, breathy whistle blew.

Jo licked her lips. And signed.

6

"I Want to Get Off!"

Their horses were waiting for them up in the sunlight—looking out for them with wide, painted eyes.

"Voilà!" murmured the old woman. "Please hurry. We are very late in starting." She watched Cecilia choose the inside horse and Jo mount the black-maned one on the outside, and nodded serenely. Then she turned her back on them and began swinging expertly around the carousel, holding on to the brass poles. "Alfred!" she called over the music. "Alfred!" A pimply youth poked his head out of a doorway set into the mirrors that circled the central engine room.

"Tell Oscar," shouted the old woman, "that we are ready."

"About time," muttered the youth in a sulky way. "This old heap'll blow up one day, waiting around like this. I told Oscar . . ."

"Alfred!"

"Okay, okay!" The boy withdrew his head.

Cecilia tittered. "What a dork," she said to Jo.

"Cecilia, don't you *realize* what we're . . ."

32

"My horse is the prettiest," said Cecilia, patting his fair, neat mane. "Look at us in the mirror." She gazed in admiration at her reflection. Jo glanced at the picture she made. It *was* pretty. A graceful, mild-looking horse, silky mane and tail barely fluttering in the breeze, and Cecilia, pink and white, astride it, holding a silken bridle.

"This wasn't so bad an idea after all, Jo," said Cecilia generously, still examining her reflection and posing this way and that.

"Cecilia, don't you . . ."

The carousel started to move.

Jo clutched at her own reins. Her horse wasn't like Cecilia's at all. It had a tumbling, untidy sort of mane, and long, thin legs. If looks were any guide, Cecilia was in for a smooth ride, and she herself was going to have a bumpy one.

She glanced quickly over her shoulder. There was still quite a crowd outside the little picket fence. A few people waved, and she waved back before turning to face the front again, feeling rather self-conscious. Mr. Angelo was sitting on the horse in front of her. He was staring straight ahead, taking no notice of the onlookers. Next to him, on the inside, sat a man in a blue shirt and brown trousers, fidgeting. In front of them was the portly figure of Mr. Milligan, the manager of the bank on the corner, looking dignified on a plump, pale horse. And beside him, perched ridiculously on a brown-spotted horse with an angry green eye and a sad, rather tattered red tail, was The Shark.

"Seven years into future time." . . . Could it possibly be true? And then, with a jolt, as if a gear had been changed, the carousel picked up speed. Jo gripped her horse's neck. Its mane felt warm under

33

her fingers. She looked quickly out toward the crowd watching on the vacant block on Marley Street. And suddenly she felt an icy shiver of fear. It was as if she'd woken from a dream into clear and frightening reality. The people had become a multicolored blur, so fast was the carousel turning. All she could hear now was the piping music, the strange, breathy carousel music with its insistent beat—faster, faster. All she could feel was the horse's coarse mane and the cold wind hard in her face.

"I want to get off!" She could hear her own voice now, yelling. But the music and the wind drowned the sound, if anyone was listening, and up and down, up and down, went her horse, tangled black mane blowing back on her fingers.

"Cecilia!" With an effort Jo forced herself to look to one side. She had made Cecilia come. It was all her fault. She had led them both into danger. She turned to Cecilia, prepared to face her frightened, angry eyes, to call out how sorry she was—even to stretch out a hand to comfort her friend, holding on as best she could with the other.

But Cecilia still sat steadily on her neat, fair horse, the reins held calmly in her smooth fingers, her face turned, smiling, to the central mirrors, while her reflection smiled back undisturbed. Jo blinked, unbelieving.

"Cecilia!" she shrieked above the wind. But Cecilia didn't stir.

Jo turned to face the front, her heart beating violently. She could see Mr. Angelo and the man in the brown trousers hunched over their horses, clinging on for dear life. And there was Mr. Milligan, slipping sideways on his plump horse, his short legs kicking at the stirrups. And The Shark, looking with

34

popping eyes over the side of the carousel, his red hair blowing violently around. He didn't look so scary now. And then she turned toward the watching crowd and heard her own voice again, screaming. For now the crowd had disappeared and the view had cleared, and life on Marley Street flicked by before her eyes, clear and bright, like a video on fast forward.

Dark, light, dark, light; people walking, talking, shopping, playing; cars rushing; trees blossoming, losing leaves, bare branched, blossoming again while she watched. It was true. It was *happening—"Seven years into future time."*

A building was pulled down, like a model, and another put up in its place. Mr. Milligan's bank on the corner grew, extended, was painted, got a grander sign. Men ran in, put up traffic lights in seconds, and retreated. More cars, more people. Faster and faster. Christmas decorations went up, came down, and minutes later went up again. Jo forgot to be frightened—forgot everything but what she was seeing. Her eyes ached and watered with staring, her brain raced. And then, just as she felt she could bear it no longer, that she would have to shut her eyes and bury her head in her horse's neck, she felt a jolt, and a change of gear, and heard the music change.

The carousel was slowing down.

7

No Time to Waste

The action on Marley Street was slowing down too. Gradually the trees stopped their frenzied tossing and jerking, grew quiet, branches clattered gently as leaves in orange and brown fluttered to the ground. Cars and people moved, hesitated, dodged one another at a pace that no longer dazzled the eyes. Around went the carousel, and bobbing gently up and down, Joanna's horse carried her away from her view of the street. In front of her Mr. Angelo and the man in the brown trousers had straightened up and were smoothing their ruffled hair and looking around them, half eager, half fearful.

"All right!"

The old man had emerged from his hut in the center of the merry-go-round and was swinging around the edge—holding on to the brass poles as the old woman had. He was grinning broadly.

"All right!" he shouted again. "Now, I'll say this once, for you lot here, and then again over on the other side. Be obliged if you'd listen carefully, so I won't have to go over it all a third time. Now, you

can get off here and have a look around. But—" He
held up his hands as a few people began to chatter
and exclaim—"But you've got to make sure you understand a few things.

"Number one: Sixty minutes we've got here, from
the moment we stop. And that's all we've got. One
hour maximum. When you hear the whistle go,
you've got ten minutes to get back here. Ten minutes only. We don't wait. Can't, as a matter of fact.
We'd lose our license like that!" He snapped his fingers.

"Number two: You don't really exist here. That
is, no one can see you. Not people, anyhow. So don't
try and talk to anyone, or make any changes, because it'll be a waste of time. And if any of you good
people get tempted to bring anything back with you,
just think again. It can't be done."

He stroked his chin and looked at them. "Every-
body clear on all that?"

Jo nodded and saw everyone else nodding too.
Even The Shark made a gesture as though he understood. Only Cecilia made no movement at all.
Plainly she had heard nothing of what had been
said. She sat peacefully on, looking at her reflection,
oblivious to the people around her and the noise of
the street.

Joanna leaned over and tugged her arm, whispered her name. But it was no good. Cecilia was lost
in some private dream. She looked quite content. But
she was missing everything! Still, maybe she'd pre-
fer it that way.

Jo heard the old man talking to the people on the
other side of the carousel. ". . . ten minutes to get
back here," he was saying. ". . . We don't wait. . . ."
The carousel still turned gently. And now Jo's horse

had come around so that she could see the street again. Marley Street. Marley Street . . . but changed.

There was a new building. She'd seen that going up. There were traffic lights on the corner. She'd seen those being installed too. The bank had almost doubled in size and looked extremely important. The trees had grown. They were quite a bit taller. And bushes and rocks ringed the vacant block, which was now obviously a proper park, with smooth green grass and wooden seats.

Across the road there was a new pizza shop, a supermarket, and a shop selling a special kind of ice cream she'd never heard of before. She could see the signs clearly from where she sat—bright and glossy.

With a grumbling squeak the carousel ground to a stop. Joanna looked around. Everyone was sitting still, staring at everyone else. She caught Mr. Angelo's eyes, and he smiled nervously at her.

"Well!" It was the old woman. She smiled tauntingly at them. "Why do you wait?" she called. "Are you not curious to see?"

She gestured with a laugh at Marley Street and watched with her hands on her hips as one by one the riders climbed stiffly down from their horses.

Jo stood by her horse and held on to its soft leather reins. She stroked its rough mane, feeling reluctant to leave its warm shelter for that unknown world outside the carousel. She glanced again at Cecilia. No, there was no help there. Cecilia would not be getting off; that was obvious.

Slouching, looking at no one, The Shark moved to the edge of the carousel. He looked out across the park to Marley Street, and his mouth tightened. He crouched a little, and jumped. And he yelled! Jo started violently, and clung closer to her friendly horse. But then she saw that everything was all right after all. The Shark was walking away from the carousel, fit and well. Walking across the vacant block, now so prettily landscaped, over the grass that by rights none of them should be treading for seven long years. He didn't look back; just kept on walking. *Into his future. Into our future!*

Suddenly everyone was rushing to the side, all fears forgotten. Suddenly they were jumping, leaping, dropping down from the carousel to the ground below, and yells, gasps, and cries floated back to Joanna, teetering on the brink. She had no choice. She had to go. She looked at the oblivious Cecilia one last time, held her breath, and jumped.

Freezing! Jo gasped and squealed as she plunged through cold air that rose around her like icy water. She hit the ground, tripped, picked herself up, and stumbled away from the carousel as fast as she could, away from the band of freezing air that surrounded it, piercing her clothes and chilling her to the bone.

With relief she felt herself break through into fresh, leafy warmth. Panting, she looked back at the carousel. The few remaining riders were jumping down to the ground now, and she heard their astonished cries as they hit the freezing air that she could now see as a gray mist that swirled around the carousel's base like a moat and rose lightly over it like a tent, making it seem to float and flicker in the sun.

And now, standing on the green grass of the vacant block, trying to pull herself together and make herself realize that this was all really happening, Jo saw that the other riders around here were also cloaked in a grey mist that floated around their bodies from head to toe, blurring shape and detail.

40

Like ghosts! Walking on Marley Street, sitting and standing around the edges of the vacant block, people chatted and went about their business without taking the slightest notice of the newcomers or the carousel. *They can't see us! We're like ghosts here.*

Joanna walked to the edge of the vacant block and moved to the pedestrian crossing near the traffic lights. She stood behind a woman in a pink dress who was holding a toddler by the hand. Mr. Angelo came up beside her. He smiled. "Take care, bambina," he whispered, and his voice was hollow and muffled as if it were coming to her from a long way away. The child in front of them wriggled his shoulders.

"I'm cold," he said to his mother, and glanced behind him. Jo held her breath, but the wide blue eyes, unfocused, looked straight through and past her. The child couldn't see her at all.

The lights changed and they crossed. As they reached the curb, Joanna stumbled as someone pushed rudely past her. It was the man in the brown trousers.

"Take it easy, man," said Mr. Angelo.

"Get a move on, then," muttered the man roughly. "I've got things to do, if you haven't."

Jo looked at him curiously and rubbed her bruised arm. He snorted and darted off to the left, pushing through the people going the other way. They obviously couldn't see him, but turned and looked at one another crossly, as though they felt themselves jostled and squeezed without knowing why. Some of them shivered and rubbed their arms and glanced upward, surprised to see that above them the sky was still blue and cloudless.

The man reached the magazine shop and disappeared inside.

Mr. Angelo looked at his watch. "I have to go quickly now," he said. "For me this is a chance to . . . to make up my mind. Even if this is a dream, I said to myself, I must make the most of the time. I don't know what I will find in my place, or how it will be. But I have to know. You know?" He paused. "No time to waste, Joanna."

"No." Joanna felt lost. She didn't really know what to do next. She watched some boys scuffling on the footpath near the bus stop, pushing each other around, yelling superhero battle cries and hurling a ball on a silver string at the shop walls. That must be some new sort of game.

"Good-bye, Joanna." Mr. Angelo was moving away. He turned and walked determinedly down Marley Street.

8

Mr. Angelo Finds Out

Jo looked around. Nothing had changed very much. The shops were a bit different. The trees were taller. Many of the people on the street were wearing clothes in bright, almost luminous, pinks, blues, and greens, and the women's skirts were longer than she was used to. But the faces were happy, or sad, or worried, or anxious, or cross, just like they were in her time, and the little kids unwillingly tagged along after their parents or pressed their noses enthusiastically against the bakery window just as they had always done.

"Give me it! Give it back!" screamed a small boy with wild black hair, and launched himself after the ball as it bounced on its silver string. The bigger boys teased him, pulling it just out of reach, making him stumble and trip over his own feet. He set his jaw and went on diving at the ball, but Jo could see that he was starting to get frustrated, embarrassed, and upset.

She turned away. She'd seen scenes like that a hundred times at school. Some people never knew when to stop.

She began to walk down the street. She knew she had to go home, even though she was afraid of what she might find there. And time was growing short.

The magazine shop had a new sign, new carpet on the floor, a toy section, and a new, younger man at the counter, but otherwise it was the same. Even the newspapers outside had a familiar ring. POP STAR DRUG RAID said one. I DIDN'T LIE CLAIMS PREZ screamed another. ELVIS SPOTTED IN DELI declared a third. Children clustered around wire baskets near the door, looking at the model cars, the activity books, and a huge pile of balls on strings. SATURDAY SPECIAL read a hastily scrawled notice. *One copy Yo-Tricks book with every Yo-Ball purchase.* Right down at the back of the shop, near a rack of greeting cards, Jo saw a gray glimmer. She squinted slightly and saw that it was the man in the brown trousers, crouching on the floor writing on a scrap of yellow paper. What on earth was he doing? She shrugged and moved on.

Behind the counter of the pharmacy, Mrs. Pickering was serving a customer. She wore what seemed to be the same mauve smock and looked as cool and collected as ever. Joanna wondered if she remembered being turned away from the carousel seven years before, and if she cared.

Through the shoe-repair-shop window she saw Mr. Brean working at his bench and occasionally casting black looks out toward the shrieking children on the sidewalk. He looked older, grayer, and crosser than ever.

The fish-and-chips shop had become a spiffy fish restaurant with flowers, little tables and chairs, and a blackboard with special dishes written on it in chalk. It didn't look as though The Shark would be very welcome there these days. Joanna wondered where he was. How was he using these precious few minutes?

45

She hadn't seen him since she had watched him walking across the grass from the carousel, though here and there she could see other riders wandering, listening, looking through their protective cloaks of mist at this world and their own future.

There was one of them now, lingering outside the fruit shop. Joanna moved closer and saw that it was Mr. Angelo. He was gently touching beautifully stacked piles of apples, pears, and oranges, admiring a box of purple grapes that were spilling over into baskets of vine leaves and figs. No wonder he looked pleased. The shop was twice as big now. It had been joined with the place next door, the little health-food store where you'd been able to buy nuts, and dried fruit, and all sorts of herbs and spices, and carob candy bars. Now all these things made a corner of the one big shop, full of people with wire baskets buying in the busy, holiday-ish Saturday-morning mood. The bright colors of the clothes added to the holiday atmosphere, and everywhere mothers and fathers scolded children as they played the ball-on-the-string game with reckless abandon. New clothes, new crazes, changed buildings—but with all that, things were much the same, Jo thought.

But who was that at the cash register? It was the lady who used to run the health-food store! Jo's heart sank. So this wasn't Mr. Angelo's place anymore. She stood hesitating at the edge of the shop. It was confusing. Why was Mr. Angelo smiling, when he must be feeling so bad?

A tall, thin man with a bushy gray beard moved up to the cash register. The health-food-store lady smiled and nodded at him and began ringing up his fruit and vegetables.

"Where's Phil today?" said the man in a friendly way as he scrabbled in his hip pocket for his wallet.

"Went off early to see the honey man," said the health-food-store lady. "He'll be back any minute—I hope!" She gestured at the line forming by the cash register and handed him his bag with a smile.

"Thanks," he said. "See you later, Mrs. Angelo."

"Barbara," she said. "Yes, see you later."

So *that* was it! Jo looked from Mr. Angelo to Barbara and back again. So *that* was in Mr. Angelo's future. Well, he looked awfully pleased about it, that was for sure. He must have liked Barbara for a long time.

There was a squeak from the back of the shop, and a dark-haired toddler in a red dress came toiling determinedly through the crowd, her chubby legs dwarfed by a bulky diaper encased in frilly short pants.

"Chrissy!" Barbara moved out from behind the cash register and bent down to the little girl, who was grinning in shy triumph with one finger in her mouth and making eyes at the people around her. "What do you think you're doing here, poppet? Mummy's busy."

"Oh!" Smiling from ear to ear, Mr. Angelo pushed forward, leaning heavily in his excitement on a bunch of especially nice grapes.

The little girl looked straight at him and squinted slightly, as if she was looking into the sunlight. "Papà?" she said hesitantly.

"Papà will be back soon, Chrissy," said Barbara. "Now look, I've got to serve these people, poppet. Where's Nonna?"

"Here I am, here. . . . Chrissy, *cara mia*, come to Nonna," called a voice from the back of the shop.

And through the crowd came the biggest surprise of all so far. A bustling, busy, talking, *smiling* old

47

Mrs. Angelo. Old as ever, dressed in black as before, but otherwise, in every way that counted, a different person, as far as Jo was concerned.

She shook her head in mock rage at Chrissy and clapped her hands.

"You run away from Nonna, eh? Want to see the shop? Want to help Mama?"

Chrissy smiled at her and held up her arms.

The two women exchanged rueful smiles.

"Well, it was a good try, Mama," said Barbara. "Phil'll be back soon, anyway." She swung the delighted child up and plumped her on the counter behind her, putting a banana in her hands to keep her busy.

Old Mrs. Angelo stepped up behind the second

cash register, and without another word they set to work again. Clutching the enormous banana, her legs stuck straight out in front of her on the counter, Chrissy watched the activity with solemn and appreciative brown eyes.

"Well!" murmured Mr. Angelo. He was quite pale.

Jo slipped out of his line of vision. She just knew he wouldn't want to be interrupted now. She moved quietly past him, keeping to the outside of the footpath. But she needn't have been so careful. Mr. Angelo was far too busy drinking in the scene that was to him the perfect ending to years of work, worry, and unhappiness to notice anything else.

9

The Best-Kept Secret

Joanna walked on down Marley Street, and falling leaves fluttered around her feet. The trees reared up on either side of the road like a guard of honor. Lots of the houses had been painted, and new shrubs in the gardens had grown, so that she had to duck under outstretched branches that now poked through iron railings and over stone walls onto the footpath.

She reached Lily Street, and her heart beat faster. So now it's my turn, she thought to herself. She clutched her hands to her chest. She didn't have her watch on and had no idea how much time had passed since she had left the carousel. Suddenly she became convinced that the hour was nearly up and that the whistle would sound before she had a chance to get home. She crossed the little road quickly and ran toward her gate.

And abruptly she stopped. She knew instantly that this house was her home no longer. Where the lavender had grown, neat brick paving encircled a small, well-clipped berry tree with ivy at its base. Fred the potted plant no longer sat waving his leaves

at the front door. Instead there was an umbrella
stand bolted to a panel on the wall below a brass
lamp. Shining brass numbers decorated the freshly
painted front door.

There was no litter of leaves on the path, no ne-
glected junk mail, rain-bedraggled and hanging
limply from the letter box. Formal, cherry-colored
curtains hung smoothly pleated at the windows. Everything was tidy, trim, organized, and totally un-
familiar.

Jo stretched out a hand and held on to one of the
iron railings of the gate. Its smooth, cold surface
brought no feeling of familiarity with it. She was
used to its old feel—half smooth, half rough, where
spots of rust broke the surface. She felt lonely, sad,
and lost, and tears filled her eyes. So that was that.
The little house was just—a little house. The house

the family used to live in. The family had moved on—and home had moved with it.

One of the red curtains twitched aside, and a comfortable-looking man with gray hair looked out. Joanna instinctively stepped back from the gate, but the man showed no sign that he'd seen her. He just looked at his neat garden with a puzzled air, and then slowly turned away.

Jo half smiled, half sobbed. Little did he know that his house was being haunted. Then she paused. And the suburb was full of riders, right now, doing the same thing she was. And maybe—probably—it had happened before. She moved away from the house thoughtfully. At Simon's gate she stopped and, without much hope, looked in. But again she was too late. The house was a family house now—not separate apartments any longer. The door stood open, and in the hallway a woman stood talking on the phone while a girl about Jo's own age stood beside her eating an apple.

Jo turned away from the gate and began slowly to walk back up Marley Street, thinking hard. Of course it had happened before. The carousel was old—the assistant, Alfred, had said that. And obviously the people who ran it had done their time-travel ride hundreds, maybe thousands, of times. She crossed Lily Street and folded her arms over her chest to protect herself from the rising, gusty wind.

She remembered that the carousel had a number— license number one hundred and forty-something. Heavens! That meant there were at least one hundred and forty others. Probably many, many more.

Then—that meant that this sort of thing—this peeping into one's future—happened to quite a few people. But somehow no one ever talked about it.

"That'd be the best-kept secret in history!" Joanna said aloud. She couldn't believe it! She looked up and saw several riders, swathed in their cloaks of mist, moving up Marley Street ahead of her. They wove in and out of the ordinary, gaily dressed shoppers, the children with their multicolored ice-cream cones and spinning balls on strings, like invisible ghosts, absolutely unnoticed.

Maybe it's always happening, thought Joanna, quickening her pace. Maybe sightseers from the past thread through and around us every day, like tourists, and we just never know it! She couldn't work out whether she found this idea frightening or exciting, and her mind turned over and over, trying to grapple with all the other questions it raised. Why were some people, like her and Mr. Angelo and Mr. Milligan the bank manager, chosen to ride, while other people, like Mrs. Pickering, were turned away? Why wasn't the whole thing known and talked about in stories, on TV, and in the newspapers? Because like any tourists, the riders would surely talk nonstop about what they'd seen and heard, once they got home. She wished now that she'd spent more time looking at the small, fine writing at the bottom of the carousel sign. Maybe it swore you to secrecy or something.

Deep in thought Jo stopped outside the fish restaurant and kicked at a pile of leaves. Well, she hadn't made much use of her time here, anyway. The visit home had been a complete anticlimax. She'd learned nothing from her adventure. Not like Simon would have done. He would have really used the chance. Not like Mr. Angelo. He'd found his future. She'd found—nothing.

Then the whistle sounded.

It was a piercing blast, and Joanna covered her

ears, screwing up her face against the terrible din. The passersby never faltered. They could hear nothing, it seemed. But hazy gray figures popped out of shops and appeared from side streets all up and down Marley Street and began making for the carousel, shimmering on its cushion of mist over at the back of the vacant block.

Joanna, hands still covering her ears, walked quickly toward the pedestrian crossing. As she reached it, the whistle stopped, to be replaced by the old, beckoning carousel music. She knew that she had ten whole minutes to get back to the carousel and there was no danger that she'd miss it—it was only a two-minute walk away now. But still she tapped her foot nervously, waiting for the lights to change. She saw the plump, misty form of Mr. Milligan slip out through the automatic doors of the bank behind an old lady with a shopping cart. He trotted across the road on his side looking very pleased with himself. No wonder. The bank was looking very big and prosperous now.

A few of the boys still played with the ball on a string by the bus stop. The little boy with black hair sat on the bus stop seat swinging his legs, watching them. He'd obviously given up trying to get the toy back.

"Go on, baby, you want it, don't you? Have a try!" yelled one of the bigger boys, flicking the ball in his direction.

The small boy ignored him and looked under his brows at the entrance to the supermarket. He was probably waiting for his father or mother and wishing they would come, but was too proud to move from the spot in search of them in front of the other boys.

The boy with the ball didn't take kindly to being ignored. He began capering around, lunging at the

54

smaller boy on the seat, spinning around and twirl-
ing the ball on its string above his head. Shoppers
brushed past him, muttering angrily as the ball
missed them by a hair. Stupid idiot, thought Jo. Stupid show-off. There'll be an accident in a minute.
She felt sorry for the little black-haired boy, who
was trying to be manly and brave about the whole
thing, but was obviously uneasy and close to tears.

The lights changed, and she stepped off the curb. She
couldn't do anything to help, even if she'd dared to take
the time. The old man had made it clear enough that it
was impossible for the riders to interfere in future time.
"You don't really exist here," he'd said.

Ahead of her, strolling happily, hands deep in his
pockets, was Mr. Angelo, and from all corners of the
vacant block other riders moved in on the carousel.
Some looked happy, some sad, some excited; some
had no expression at all. The Shark was already
back, slouching beside his horse, talking to the assistant, Alfred. Alfred seemed to be complaining:
kicking at a splintered board on the carousel floor,
gesturing contemptuously with his thumb at the
central mirrored engine room, where Jo could hear
machinery grinding away under the sound of the
music. And there was Cecilia, still peacefully lost in
her own reflection. With a shock Jo realized that
she'd forgotten all about Cecilia.

She held her breath and plunged into the mist
swirling about the carousel base. Shutting her eyes
tightly against the aching cold, she clambered up to
the platform with numbing fingers. She reached her
horse, climbed aboard, and patted the wild, dark mane.
The horse seemed to look back at her in a friendly,
welcoming way. She sat and waited while in twos and
threes the riders returned to the carousel.

10

Stowaway

The old man popped his head out of the mirrored door. He wiped crumbs from his mustache with the back of his hand and began swinging around the carousel, checking the riders. He stopped and leaned on the empty horse next to Mr. Angelo.

"Seen your friend?" he said to The Shark and Mr. Angelo. The Shark shrugged and looked away.

"No friend of mine," he muttered.

"He's cutting it a bit fine, anyhow," said the old man, grinning and shaking his head.

Jo saw a hazy figure in the distance and sat up straight on her horse. "Here he comes," she said, pointing.

Sure enough, the man in the brown trousers was puffing toward them across the grass. He reached the carousel and clambered aboard. The old man nodded to him. "Just made it, buddy," he said, and chuckled. "Had a busy time, did you?"

The man nodded curtly and awkwardly climbed onto his horse, pulling a handkerchief from his pocket and wiping his red forehead and cheeks. Some pieces of yellow paper fluttered to the ground as the handkerchief unfolded, and with an exclamation of annoyance and a furtive look around, he retrieved them and stuffed them back in his pocket.

"You all right then?" said the old man rather coolly. "Got everything?"

The man looked at him. "Yes, thanks," he muttered, looking away. But his hand stole to his pocket as he spoke, and his fingers dipped into it as though to assure himself that something was still there.

The old man sniffed, and then grinned.

"Good!" he said. "Nothing to stop us, then." He turned his back. "Okay this side, Mrs. D.!" he shouted.

The old woman appeared from the other side of the carousel. "And here," she called.

"Alfred!" roared the old man. "Let her go!"

And with a creak and a groan of old gears, the carousel began to move.

Jo patted her horse's mane. Here we go again, she thought, her back prickling. Cecilia gazed on into the mirror, unmoved. She'll have a stiff neck when she gets off, thought Jo. She settled herself more comfortably as her horse moved sedately on, taking her around to the other side of the circle, away from the street.

It was then that she heard the crash. Breaking glass, screams, and a bellow of rage. Coming from Marley Street. She twisted in the saddle but could see only the community center next door sailing by, then the fence that separated the vacant block from the house behind it.

"It'll be those kids, bet you," growled the man in the brown trousers to Mr. Angelo. "Young hooligans."

And as the carousel moved them on, they saw that
he was right. Even at that distance they could see
the jagged hole in Mr. Brean's shop window, could
see boys scattering through the crowded street. And
then they saw Mr. Brean himself, in a towering rage,
tear over the pedestrian crossing and onto the vacant block, in hot pursuit of a small figure whose
skinny legs and pumping arms worked as though
the devil himself was on his heels.

Jo recognized the boy she'd seen at the bus stop.
He *would* be the one to get caught. For sure the
broken window wasn't his doing at all. But it looked
as though he was going to pay for it.

"Stop, you young guttersnipe!" yelled Mr. Brean.
"I'll get the cops onto you. See how you like that!
Wait till I catch you. . . . I'll shake every tooth out
of your cheeky head!"

Run, Jo begged the boy silently. Don't fall. Now

her horse was almost straight in front of the small racing figure. She could see that he was tiring, and that Mr. Brean was catching up.

The boy looked up, his face desperate and tear-stained. He glanced over his shoulder.

Don't look back, thought Jo. Come on! And at that moment the boy looked forward again, and ran straight for her, eyes wide with fright.

Jo didn't think. She didn't hesitate. She jumped from her horse, leaned over the side of the carousel, put her arms out, and with a gasp caught the small body and swung it up, to safety.

"Joanna!" cried Phil Angelo. "Don't!"

The little boy stared at Jo, speechless. She put him on her horse and sat behind him, shielding him with her jacket. She looked defiantly at Mr. Angelo. Adults always stuck together in the end—bad and good alike.

But Mr. Brean had stopped dead and was gazing around in utter bewilderment. The carousel was picking up speed. Around they went again, and in that full circle Jo began to realize what she had done.

The boy whimpered. "I want my mummy," he said, and began to cry.

Jo stared straight ahead, her heart pounding, her cheeks hot. She saw, on the next turn, that Mr. Brean was wandering back across the grass, shaking his head and looking back over his shoulder every few steps, as though he expected his quarry to somehow reappear as abruptly as he'd vanished.

But Jo, looking over the child's head at Mr. Angelo's troubled face, and the sneering glances of the man in the brown trousers, could take no joy in Mr. Brean's confusion. The carousel music piped wildly, the world outside picked up speed. There was no way, now, that anyone could get off.

Holding for dear life to the horse's mane, the boy turned his tense, frightened face to hers. His lip trembled.

"I don't like it on here," he wailed loudly. "This merry-go-round goes too fast. It wasn't in the park before. I want to see my daddy. I should wait for my daddy outside the shop. He'll be cross with me. And Brett took the Yo-Ball. It's the special one. The number one. I wasn't supposed to have it." Tears began running down his cheeks.

"It's okay," said Joanna helplessly. "Daddy won't be cross. It's not your fault."

It's my fault, she thought. My fault. Oh, what will I do?

"What's your name?" she said. "Don't cry." She patted his arm awkwardly.

The boy sniffed. "Davy," he said. "I'm Davy, and I'm six years old, and I live at forty-eight Singer Street. Can I go home now?"

"Soon," Joanna promised wildly.

The boy gave a shuddering sigh and looked fearfully around him, clutching the horse's neck with all his might. The world outside the carousel had become a blur. The wind beat into their faces.

And then the music began to falter.

It was as though someone was poking a stick into the works of a music box. Little gaps and jerks, tinkles and thuds, broke into the steady rhythm. Something was very wrong. The carousel shuddered once, twice, three times, and with every shudder there was a rumbling from the engine room. Head down, frantically gripping the little stowaway and her horse, too, Joanna heard over the racket the cries of the other riders, the shouts from the old man and the old woman, the panicking, high-pitched yells of Alfred, grappling, one imagined, with the machinery inside the engine room.

Then, with a shrieking clash of sound and a sickening jolt, it was all over. Silence. The carousel spun gently, freely, for one half circle, and then, with a sigh of old timber, it ground softly to a stop.

Joanna lifted her head and looked quickly and fearfully over the side. She saw a blurred picture of

Marley Street. Marley Street, with its shops, its people, its trees, dead still. Nothing moved. Not a leaf, or a shadow. It was like a video when someone has pushed the pause button, or like a film frozen at a single moment. Everything was wispy around the edges, faint and blurred. And there was no sound at all. Like an elevator stuck between floors, the carousel sat dumb, useless, and inert while its passengers looked at one another in growing panic, knowing they were trapped and helpless.

11

The Shark to the Rescue

The central door flew open, and the old woman appeared, scowling. Her monkey-paw hands grasped the brass poles as she swung herself up and around the carousel.

"Stay seated, riders, if you please," she commanded. She needn't have worried about that, really, because everyone was far too terrified and bewildered to move.

She addressed them sternly. "We have a problem," she announced. "A most serious problem. At present we are unknowing of the cause, but no doubt it will be discovered soon. In the meantime, it is of the utmost importance that you do not attempt to leave the carousel. This would be extremely dangerous. *Comprenez?* Understand?"

The terrified riders nodded and tightened their grip on their horses.

The old man appeared, wiping his forehead with an oil-stained red handkerchief. She looked at him with close attention, but he shook his head, shrugged, and went back inside.

"So," she said. "It seems we are still mystified. But please do not distress yourselves."

"Look, are you saying we're stuck here, or what?" It was the man in the brown trousers. He stuck his chin out and stared aggressively at the woman.

She stared back at him, her black eyes narrow. "For the moment, monsieur, yes," she said. "It is unfortunate, but—"

"Unfortunate!" he growled. "Unfortunate! I should say it is unfortunate. It's a disgrace, that's what it is. This stupid ride's obviously a complete crock. Unsafe. You'll be hearing from me, I can tell you, if and when we get back in one piece. You'll be hearing from my lawyers!"

"Oh, dry up," grunted The Shark, looking at him in disgust. "We're all in the same boat."

"Ah!" The woman almost smiled at The Shark, half-closing her eyes. "The monsieur must do whatever he thinks best. But for now I must concentrate on the problem at hand." Her narrow gaze swept over the horses and riders before her, swept past Mr. Angelo and Cecilia and—Jo, with Davy clasped in her arms. Her eyelids flew up. "Oscar!" she shrieked. "Oscar! Alfred!"

The heads of the two men popped out of the door.

She pointed to Jo and Davy with a shaking, be-ringed finger. "That boy!" she cried. "He shouldn't be here. He is not a rider."

"What!" exclaimed the old man.

"That's it then," said Alfred gloomily. He swung onto the platform and came to stand behind Jo, hands in his pockets.

"Where did he come from?" demanded the old man. "Strike me lucky! I can't believe this!"

"He—he—was being chased, and he just . . . got on," quavered Jo.

They looked at her in silence, and she felt her cheeks grow hot. "Well—um—I did help him . . . a bit," she said finally.

"Never seen that happen before," said the old man. "Have you, Mrs. D.?"

"Two times only," said the old woman. She looked at Jo and Davy. "It is very rare."

"Anyhow," muttered Alfred grumpily, "what's it matter? The point is, the old wreck's been overloaded. That's why it's blown a gasket." He kicked at the nearest horse. "The new models've got automatic cutout. Told you this thing was only fit for the scrap heap."

Mrs. D. looked at him coldly. "Alfred, do not speak like that," she said sternly. "Have a little loyalty."

"Aw, rats!" said Alfred.

"You mind your tongue, Alfred!" roared Oscar, suddenly losing his temper. "You get down there and get working, boy!"

"Yeah!" yelled the man in the brown trousers. "Get the thing fixed and cut the chat, will you?"

"That does it!" Alfred tore the oily rag from his hip pocket and threw it to the ground. "That's it! I'm sick and tired of it. I'm just taken for granted, that's what I am. Alfred this! Alfred that! Alfred the other! Nursemaid to a heap of junk. And now every Tom, Dick, and Harry thinks he can give me orders. A man'd be a fool to stick with it, and I'm not going to. So put that in your pipe and smoke it!"

He jumped down from the platform and bounded through the doorway into the engine room. Mrs. D. and Oscar looked at each other.

65

Alfred reappeared with a small bag in one hand and a cardboard box in the other.

"Don't be foolish, Alfred!" said Mrs. D. calmly.

"Listen here, boy . . ." began the old man.

"I'm fed up with listening. I'm off!" said Alfred.

"What about us?" exploded the man in the brown trousers. "We'll be stuck here for good. You can't do it!"

"You just watch me!" yelled Alfred.

And in paralyzed silence they did watch as he leaped over the side of the carousel. They saw him walk steadily away, the only moving thing in the blurred, silent landscape. Soon he was just a hazy dot, and then they could see him no more.

The old woman put her hands to her head. "La, la!" she lamented. "Now, Oscar, what are we to do?

66

Never, never have I seen such behavior. For a grade-two carousel mechanic to abandon his post. It is unheard of! It cannot be done!"

"Well, it has been done, Mrs. D., it seems," said the old man. "They should never've given the grade twos between-zone travel capacity. I told them. They'll listen next time, won't they?" He paused. "If there is a next time," he muttered. He bent his head and ran his fingers through his hair.

Then an idea seemed to strike him.

"Anyone here," he called hopefully, "a mechanic, or an engineer, or works with machinery or anything?"

Silence. People looked at one another, shaking their heads.

He dashed around to the other side of the carousel and they heard him repeating the question.

Again there was silence.

"Ah—he is a dreamer!" Mrs. D. cast up her eyes and spread her hands out in front of her. She laid her hand on the neck of Jo's horse. "My old faithful, my carousel," she murmured. "I am sorry."

"You're sorry," snapped the man in the brown trousers. "Never mind this pile of old junk! What about us?"

Mr. Milligan, on the horse in front of him, sighed deeply. "It would help if you would keep your temper," he said disapprovingly.

"Yeah. Why don't you pipe down, buddy!" said The Shark grimly. He jumped off his horse and slouched to the old woman's side. She looked up at him, puzzled. "I'll have a go," he said.

"That's a good one," sneered the man in the brown trousers. "I like your nerve. You wouldn't know where to start. You'd get us into a worse mess than we're in already. I know him, lady. Everyone here knows him. A hopeless case if ever there was one."

"I'm good with cars. I like old machines." The Shark brought out the words hesitantly, almost as if he were shy.

The old woman looked into his eyes for a few seconds, then nodded as if satisfied.

"Very good," she said briskly. "I should not have doubted. I must confess I wondered why you came. Now my question is answered. Please come with me."

12

Waiting

"What's happening?" asked Davy fearfully.

"They're fixing the merry-go-round," said Jo, staring at the closed door behind which The Shark and the old people had vanished.

"When it's fixed, can I go home?"

Jo hesitated. The pointed face with its dark brown eyes looked at her trustingly. "Oh, yes," she said, swallowing. "Don't worry, Davy. You just sit quietly."

He nodded, pressing his lips together and looking to the front again. He plucked at the horse's mane with nervous, grubby fingers.

Mr. Angelo and the man in the brown trousers had gotten off their horses and were pacing up and down, stretching their legs. The man was grumbling and complaining. Mr. Angelo was looking worried.

"And what if they don't get it going again, eh? Where does that leave us?" said the man.

Mr. Angelo glanced at Jo, Davy, and Cecilia to see

if they had heard. "Shh," he said. "You'll scare the kids, going on like that, pal."

The man scowled. "Look, Phil, I can't be worried about that. Maybe you've got nothing to get back home for, but I have, I can tell you."

Mr. Angelo shook his head. "I have a very good reason to get back . . . now," he said.

The man looked at him curiously. "You found out something useful, did you, back there?" he said. "What was it, if I may ask?"

Mr. Angelo turned his head away. "Oh—just that things are going to go well for me. Worth working for," he murmured.

"That's fine, Phil," said the man, smiling rather scornfully. "So we're both going to strike it lucky."

"You had good news too?"

The man laughed. "Didn't bother with all that, Phil. Sure, I was having a few problems. Wondering which way to go to sort myself out. But look, a chance like this doesn't come every day, does it? And I've never been one for sitting back and waiting for things to happen. My idea is to make them happen. So . . ." He glanced at the bank manager and dropped his voice, and Jo, eavesdropping from behind them, had to strain to hear his next words. "I shouldn't tell you this, Phil," muttered the man, "but you're not the type to turn a man in, and anyway, frankly, who'd believe you? I tell you what I did. I went straight to the magazine shop and stayed there till I heard the whistle blow." He looked at Mr. Angelo expectantly and bit his thumb.

Mr. Angelo blinked at him. "Sorry," he said at last. "I must have missed something. I don't quite . . ."

"The magazine shop, pal," hissed the man. "I spent my hour tucked up with every newspaper around the place. Papers with news seven years from now. You see? I wrote down every horse that had won a race, the winning lotto and keno numbers that week—all that. Now I know those results for certain. Who said there was no such thing as a safe bet? I can't lose."

He grinned triumphantly at Mr. Angelo, who was looking rather bewildered and taken aback.

"Once I'm home, see," he said, "bang, into the safe goes this little lot." He pulled out the yellow sheets of paper from his pocket and waved them under Mr. Angelo's nose. "Seven years later—bang, out they come again, see? I use the info to make a few bets, and bang for the third and last time—I'm a millionaire. Get the picture?"

"Ah—is that *allowed?*" said Mr. Angelo, after a short silence. "I thought . . ."

The man's feverish face grew flat and grim in a moment.

"I don't know anything about it being allowed or not allowed, Phil. They said don't pick up anything and bring it back—well, I used the backs of some old receipts I had, see?" He waved the yellow papers. "As far as I'm concerned, anything I wrote on them's my business. If other people weren't bright enough to think of the same idea, that's their bad luck. No good them turning around and being peeved after the event!"

"Ah—I wasn't . . ." Mr. Angelo began. But the man turned his back, stuffing the yellow papers deep into his pocket, and stalked off through the painted horses, his shoulders hunched in cold anger.

"Mr. Angelo's face looks funny," said Davy.

"What?"

"His face. It's funny."

"Davy, shh . . ."

"It *is*, it *is* funny. His beard on his mouth is gone."

"You mean a mustache?"

"Mustache. Yes. How did it get cut off?"

"It didn't get cut off. . . . Um . . . he hasn't grown it yet."

"What?"

"Never mind. I didn't know you knew Mr. Angelo."

"We go to his shop. I go with my mummy and daddy. He has a baby called Chrissy."

"I know."

"And he has a granny. She gave me some grapes,

72

you know." Suddenly Davy's lip trembled again."I'm hungry. I want to go home."

"Soon we'll go home." Jo put her arm around his waist. "Don't worry. I'm here. I'll look after you."

She looked around helplessly. She could hear bangs and clangs from inside the mirrored engine room, but there was no sign yet that The Shark and Oscar had made any progress. The other riders talked softly together. Mr. Angelo leaned against his horse, staring into space. Beside her, Cecilia sat on her prim, fair horse and gazed blissfully at her reflection. Jo shivered. Beyond the carousel, the fuzzy stillness of Marley Street hung like a silent cloud.

13

The Riders Decide

Davy slept, his head bent over the horse's mane. He was heavy on Jo's arm, but she didn't try to pull it away, in case she woke him. At least asleep, he wasn't feeling worried and homesick. She hoped he'd sleep for a long time. She closed her own eyes. Then she felt a hand on her shoulder and jumped.

"Now listen to me, *ma petite!*" It was the old woman, murmuring. "We must decide what to do about your small friend here."

"Is the carousel fixed?" asked Jo.

"Not yet, no, it is not. But I have hopes. Charles is clever. Already he is more help than the wretched Alfred. He has a feeling for the old machinery—one can tell that straight away. But against the time when we can leave, we must make a plan."

"We . . . we can just take him home, can't we? And then go home ourselves? Now that Alfred's gone. I mean, I've been thinking—there aren't too many people on board anymore, and so . . ."

"It is not that simple. The carousel—we may get it going again, but this will be only a temporary

74

measure. First aid only, you understand? It has had a severe breakdown, this old machine, and needs careful and thorough attention in the workshop. The prudent thing to do would be to return to your time as soon as we can do so. Otherwise . . . well, Oscar and I cannot answer for the consequences."

"Well, that's it, then, isn't it?" chipped in the man in the brown trousers, who had been listening. "The boy had no business getting on here to start with. We can't be penalized for one naughty kid's bit of nonsense."

The old woman looked at him, and at the other riders who had gathered around. "The problem is, monsieur," she said, "that this child is clearly not yet seven years old. That is correct, is it not, *ma petite?*"

Jo nodded. "He said he was six."

"So . . ." The old woman put out a wrinkled brown finger and gently touched the sleeping boy's rough black hair. "If we take him back to your own time, you see, we will not only be taking him away from his family and the little life he knows, which would be crime enough, for he would be a small ghost in your time, as you are in his. We may be taking him away from life itself. We will be taking him back to a time before his birth. There is no guarantee that he will not simply disappear and exist no more."

The riders looked at one another.

"What are you suggesting we do, then?" asked Mr. Milligan, looking worried.

"I am thinking we should try to return him, as the girl asks. But in full knowledge of the risk," said the old woman gravely.

"Well, I'm sorry," said the man in the brown trousers aggressively. "I don't agree with this. There are

75

more of us. You're saying we should risk the whole kit and caboodle for one kid who might be quite okay anyway. I vote we just go back."

"We can't do that," cried Jo. "He might die!"

The man looked irritated and embarrassed. "Look, sweetie, it's not nice to think about, I know, but it wouldn't hurt him or anything, would it, lady?" He appealed to Mrs. D. "He'd just fade away. It'd be like he never existed at all. Isn't that about it?"

The old woman nodded, and he spread his hands. "There you are, you see?" he said.

A few people murmured agreement.

"That is your decision then?" said the old woman calmly.

Mr. Angelo spoke. "I think we should take him back," he said firmly. The man in the brown trousers shot a venomous look at him, and he flinched but went on. "I would not like to think," he said, "of . . . of a child of mine in this boy's place and no one willing to help. Would any of you?" He turned and looked at the other riders. One by one they shook their heads.

"Certainly not," said Mr. Milligan firmly. "We should definitely take him back. It would be outrageous to think otherwise."

"Sentimental claptrap!" snorted the man in the brown trousers. He turned on Mr. Milligan. "Call yourself a businessman! What a joke. Rinky-dink little show, your bank. I know. Only reason it grew was the Yo-Ball company banking with you because you took a chance for once in your life and lent it the dough to get started. I read all about it back there. Pathetic! If you think I'll ever put my money with you, you've got another think coming, buddy.

And as for you, Angelo—you haven't even got a kid. What are you going on about?"

Jo opened her mouth to correct him, but shut it again. It was Mr. Angelo's secret, after all.

"Let's vote on it!" called a girl at the back of the crowd. "That's the fairest way."

"*Bien,*" said the old woman. "Good. All in favor of taking Davy home?"

Jo raised her hand and looked anxiously at the others. One by one the arms went up until only the man in the brown trousers and two other people were left standing grim faced and surrounded.

"You're all mad. Have it your own way, then!" shouted the man in the brown trousers furiously. He elbowed his way through the crowd and, finding nowhere to storm off to, had to be content with climbing back on his horse and sitting, shoulders hunched, with his back to them.

There was a shout from the engine room. The carousel gave a shudder and a lurch, and began to hum.

The mirrored door flew open.

"He's done it, Mrs. D.!" It was Oscar, jumping with excitement, a huge black smear of oil daubing one cheek. "Charlie's got her going! The boy's a beauty!"

"Riders—to your places," ordered the old woman. "Oscar—it is decided. We take the boy back."

The old man grinned and touched two fingers to his forehead in a mock salute. "Nothing ventured, nothing gained, I always say," he yelled, over the rising sound of machinery. He looked back over his shoulder. "Charlie!" he roared into the engine room. "It's a goer. Let her rip!"

78

Jo clutched her horse's mane, feeling between her arms the soft warmth of the sleeping boy. He stirred.

"You're on your way home, Davy," she murmured in his ear.

The carousel began to move, and the music rose. Jo held on and shut her eyes.

14

"Won't I See You Anymore?"

"Hey!" Davy was pulling at her hand. "Hey, please!"

Jo opened her eyes and blinked. The carousel was slowing down. She looked out at Marley Street. Everything was in focus again, and everything was moving. Leaves fell, dogs yapped, people jostled each other, and cars jerked forward as the traffic lights changed. It was marvelous.

Davy wriggled. "I want to get down now," he said.

Jo climbed stiffly from her horse. It regarded her with a warning black eye. She put her hands under Davy's arms and heaved him carefully down.

The old woman appeared beside them as the carousel came to a stop.

"*Bien*. Now, *mon enfant*, you must run home," she said to Davy, bending down toward him. "Come, and I will help you down to the ground. Be quick, now."

Davy looked at her bright, fierce eyes and at the monkey-paw hands stretched out to him and shrank back against Jo, fumbling for her hand.

"Come along, little one!" insisted Mrs. D. "We cannot wait for long."

He stared at her, speechless.

"I'll help you down, Davy," said Jo, glancing apologetically at Mrs. D. "There's nothing to be scared of. You can go back to the seat and wait for your dad."

"That, unfortunately, he cannot do, I think," said Mrs. D. slowly. "We have done our best, but alas, we have not been able to arrive at exactly the same time as before. Our instruments are not working accurately. We are an hour late. I fear that Davy's *papà* will have found him missing and returned home to start a search by now."

Jo felt Davy's hand give a little jerk. She bent toward him.

"It's okay, Davy," she said. "You can just walk home, and your mum and dad will be there waiting."

Davy, still staring at the old woman's glittering eyes, burst into tears. "I can't go home by myself," he sobbed. "I'm not allowed to cross the roads. I'm too little. Mummy said. I can't go home! I want to see my mummy!" His voice rose to a wail.

"Davy, this is foolish. If you want to see *maman,* you must go yourself. Come now." The old woman reached for him. He screamed, turned, and clutched at Jo's waist.

"You take me," he begged. "You take me home."

Joanna looked at Mrs. D., who was shaking her head. Over Mrs. D.'s head she could see The Shark and Oscar, who had come out of the engine room and were standing, watching. The Shark turned and said something to the old man, who raised his eyebrows, shrugged, nodded, and made his way toward them.

"Charlie says he reckons we can hold for fifteen minutes or so," he said to Mrs. D. in a low voice.

She turned to him, frowning.

"We are taking enough risks," she said.

"May as well give it a go, I reckon, Mrs. D.," he said.

She looked at him for a moment, then nodded and turned quickly.

"Go with him," she said to Jo. "As he has been with you here, I believe you will be visible to him out there, for a time, at least. Go, and as quickly as you can, return. When you hear the whistle, you will know you have minutes only. Do you understand? Are you willing?"

Jo nodded, a lump in her throat.

"Go!" said the old woman.

Jo grabbed Davy's hands, and pulled him around to face Marley Street. "Ready?" she said. She looked around and saw the reassuring nod of Mr. Angelo, the worried face of Mr. Milligan, the scowl of the man in the brown trousers, Cecilia serenely contemplating the mirrors. She turned back, took a deep breath.

"Jump!" she shouted, and together she and Davy jumped.

At a trot they crossed the vacant block.

"What number on Singer Street was it again, Davy?" asked Jo. She glanced at his strained, tear-stained face. He could see her, all right. That was one blessing, at least.

"Forty-eight. Forty-eight Singer Street, I live at."

"All right. Come on, then. We've got to hurry."

"Wait!"

They spun around to see the round, mist-swathed form of Mr. Milligan jogging toward them. He arrived, puffing and blowing. His sleek hair flopped over his forehead, and his tie had blown over one shoulder.

"Your ball . . ." he panted. "You lost your ball, didn't you, son?"

Davy looked at Jo, and tightened his grip on her hand.

"I heard you say . . . your special ball. Taken," panted Mr. Milligan.

"The special Yo-Ball. The number one!" Davy's eyes widened. "I forgot! It's not my one. I forgot. Oh, no. . . . She'll be so cross with me. . . ." His voice rose to a wail.

"No, no, it's all right." Mr. Milligan looked confused and rubbed his wet forehead helplessly with his handkerchief. He spoke rapidly to Jo, pointing to a trash can at the corner of the park, near the traffic lights. "I just saw, just then, that young lout who was teasing the boy run by and throw something in that trash can. Something caught the light. The silver string, it was, I'm sure."

"Oh, thank you, Mr. Milligan," cried Jo. They hurried over to the trash can and looked inside. Sure enough, a rather battered ball lay shimmering in a nest of wastepaper and ice-cream sticks. Davy fished it out, speechless with delight, and clutched it to his chest as though it were precious treasure.

"All the children seem to have them," said Mr. Milligan to Jo. "They're everywhere. I gather my bank profits mightily from the whole business." He lifted his chin. "It seems old stick-in-the-mud Milligan made a smart decision somewhere along the way. Anyway, it's not as if"—he lowered his voice— "it's not as if the little chap couldn't have gotten a new one easily enough. But he seemed to think his

was special, and he might have been upset about it, mightn't he?"

Jo nodded, and smiled at the nervous bank manager, who seemed so apologetic about letting his tender heart show for once.

"Well, well, you'd better get on now, dear," urged Mr. Milligan anxiously. "Time's short, apparently. Lord!" He mopped at his forehead again. "For a man who never takes chances, I've lashed out today, haven't I? I thought nothing on earth would get me off that carousel till we were safely home. Go on, now, get along—and hurry back!"

Jo urged the little boy on, down Marley Street and across the first side street, ignoring the passersby who turned and stared. They couldn't see her, but of course they could see Davy, and a few motherly-looking women paused as if to try to stop him and find out what such a small boy was doing stumbling down the main street, tear-stained and grubby and apparently alone.

They crossed the second side street, ran to the corner, and turned left on to Singer Street.

"It's nearly here!" cried Davy. His legs were almost buckling under him.

"Eighty-four, eighty-two, eighty . . ." Jo read the numbers feverishly.

"My legs hurt," complained Davy, hanging back heavily on her hand.

"Davy, *please*. You have to hurry. Please! I've got to get back to the carousel."

Sixty-four, sixty-two, sixty, fifty-eight . . .

Trees overhung the footpath, dropping leaves into the soft piles already heaped around their trunks. Their feet crackled and brushed the leaves aside.

"Fifty . . . forty-eight! Is this it?"

Davy was beaming. He pushed open the gate and ran up the path, kicking aside the rustling brown leaves. Lavender bent and sprang back as he passed, and the smell drifted back to Jo, waiting at the gate.

The door of the house stood open, and in the front room someone was playing the piano. The soft chords floated out into the silent street—soft, beautiful music that somehow made Jo feel sad and excited, both at the same time. How wonderful, to be able to make music like that.

"Come on!" Davy was standing on the front step and looking back at her. A dog began barking inside the house.

Jo shook her head. She had to go. But still she lingered. Somehow, despite all the trouble he'd been, she didn't want to leave the little black-haired boy.

85

Davy seemed to feel the same way. He stared at her, then ran back down the path and grabbed her hand.

"I have to go back, Davy." She crouched down to give him a hug. "You go inside now."

"Can you come back another day and take me to your house?" he asked confidently, patting her shoulder.

She shook her head. "I live too far away," she said. She looked down the path, through the plumes of lavender, at the mossy front steps, and up to the front door, where a potted plant stood waving its rather tattered-looking leaves in the breeze. Her eyes widened. What . . . ?

"Won't I see you anymore?" said Davy.

Suddenly Jo was gripped by a powerful feeling that shook her whole body. She grabbed Davy's shoulders and looked deeply into his face.

"What's the matter?" Davy wriggled and looked back at her curiously.

"I'm . . . It's just that . . . I'm okay. But you'd better go in and tell . . . tell your mum that you're home. She'll be worried. She'll . . . be worried."

The barking grew louder, and suddenly there was a blur of black ears and legs, and a flurry of excited paws on the stairs. Davy turned, and his face broke into an adoring grin.

"Podgy!"

With a yelp Podge ran stiffly down the path, ears flapping dangerously, swinging at the lavender. She threw herself into Davy's arms.

Jo stood rooted to the spot, a hand over her mouth. Suddenly everything seemed to be moving very slowly. She saw a familiar figure run out to the top of the stairs.

"Mummy!" Davy was racing toward the figure.

"Davy, Davy, where have you been? Daddy's been looking . . . Jo, Jo, he's here!"

Joanna saw Podge cock her head and gaze in her direction with puzzled spaniel eyes. She heard the piano music stop, and saw a tall, black-haired figure pull aside the curtains of the front window, leaning forward until she could almost see . . .

The whistle blew.

Jo took one last look, turned, and ran.

15

The Fine Print

Up Marley Street with its taller trees dropping the same yellow leaves, across the busy road where cars and brightly clad pedestrians jostled, onto the vacant block, now a green-grassed park where the children played with balls on silver strings ... head spinning, chest hurting, ears ringing with the whistle sound, Jo ran to the carousel.

She felt rather than saw thin brown arms reach down and lift her up, up, to the cheers of the waiting riders.

"Hoopla!" The old woman helped her onto her horse and smiled at her with raised eyebrows. "So," she said. "Success?" Jo nodded, breathless. The woman cocked her head and her eyes twinkled. "You found more than you bargained for on ... Singer Street, yes?"

"Yes," said Jo.

"It was not good-bye, but *au revoir,* is that not so?"

"What?"

"Mrs. D., are we right? This is getting really dicey!" Oscar stood waving at the engine-room door.

"Okay, Oscar. We're all right."

"Charlie, let her rip! And cross your fingers, son."

The music rose. The carousel began to turn.

Jo stared straight ahead.

Au revoir . . . to meet again.

It was that noise from Marley Street that finally roused Jo. She raised her head from her horse's neck and looked around her. They had made it! Charlie, Oscar, and Mrs. D. had brought them home. The carousel swung, whispering, one half turn, and stopped.

Dry eyed, Jo drank in the sight. Gone were the traffic lights, the new buildings and signs. Mr. Milligan's bank had shrunk back to its normal, modest size and was firmly closed, as usual on Saturday morning. The neatly landscaped park was just a vacant block again, and children played ordinary games on the rough grass, leaping and jumping against the wind.

My time. My home. But anywhere the people I love are, is home. Any time where I am, is my time.

"Much to learn in one morning, eh?" Mrs. D. stood smiling at her horse's head, and patted its nose.

Jo shook her head. "I'll never forget it!" she said.

Mrs. D. wagged a skinny, be-ringed finger at her.

"Ah," she said. "You riders—you are all the same. You never read the fine print."

She laughed and was gone.

Cecilia yawned and turned her head. "What a bore!" she groaned, and stretched her arms above her head.

"Cecilia!"

"What's up? Come on, let's go and get a drink."

"Cecilia, you've got no idea what's been happening!"

"Jo, stop acting weird, will you? We've been riding on a kids' merry-go-round, that's what's been happening."

The old man swung around to them, holding on to the brass poles. "Thank you . . . thank you. . . . Please dismount safely, riders. Good luck to you. . . . Good luck and good-bye."

"Come on, Jo."

They climbed down from their horses.

"Mine was the prettiest," said Cecilia, heading for the exit sign. Jo looked back at her gangling horse, with its wild black mane and humorous, painted eye, and nodded.

"But mine was more interesting," she said.

In the tent the riders mingled and milled, each strangely unwilling, it seemed, to be the first to leave. Jo could see Mr. Angelo by the entrance. He looked different. The sad, worried lines had left his face, leaving it calm, with a beam of hope and expectation lighting his smile. He caught Jo's eye and lifted a hand in greeting. Jo waved back and looked around for The Shark. She wanted to thank him for what he had done. She wasn't scared of him anymore. But he was nowhere to be seen.

The old man pushed through the crowd and pulled open the tent flap. Bright light streamed in. There was no one outside. Not one curious onlooker peered through the opening to the riders inside. The only people on the vacant block now were the playing children, and they seemed to have forgotten that the carousel was there.

"This way, ladies and gentlemen, please!" called

the old man. "This way!" He nodded and grinned at the people as they filed past him. "Happy days!" he said to one and another as they said good-bye.

Cecilia and Jo were the last to go.

"Thank you," said Jo, looking into his bright eyes. What else was there to say?

Oscar grinned at her and rubbed his chin. "All in a day's work," he said.

Jo hesitated. "I was looking for The Sha—for Charlie."

"Ah," said the old man. "Seems he's decided to stay on with us for a bit. Nice boy, Charlie. Good mechanic. Not much for him out there, is there?" He gestured at the world outside. "We'll look after him, Mrs. D. and me will."

He held the tent flap open. "But you're a different kettle of fish, little lady. Off you go, and get into it!"

Jo smiled, nodded, and stepped out, with Cecilia, into the sunlight.

"Cecilia, I've got to tell you . . ." Jo paused. How *could* she tell Cecilia? *What* could she tell her? She tried to organize her thoughts.

They walked on across the grass of the vacant block. All around them the other riders walked too.

"Well, what is it?" snapped Cecilia impatiently. She wriggled her neck and shoulders irritably. "I feel so stiff!" she complained. "I feel as if I've been sitting on that horse for hours!"

"That's because . . ." Jo stopped walking. "Because . . ." She shook her head. "It's funny, I know it, but I just can't . . ." Memories hovered at the edge of her mind, tantalizing, impossible to grasp and put into words. I'm forgetting! Forgetting! No! she

thought. I've got to remember. I've got to tell Mum, Dad, Simon. . . . I've got to remember for *me*. But the harder she tried to catch the memories, the farther they retreated.

Back in the tent Oscar, Mrs. D., and Charlie Murphy, alias The Shark, watched the riders stop walking, one by one.

"Here we go," said Oscar, with a grin. "Look at them fighting it, will you?"

Mrs. D. shook her head. "The sign makes it perfectly clear that they should not expect to remember with their conscious minds. After all, they must realize what

complications and difficulties that would cause. And yet forever and always, our riders, they . . ."

"Oh, go on, Mrs. D. You *know* they never read the fine print! C'mon, let's get ourselves a cup of tea. You too, Charlie. I'm parched!"

"What's the *matter* with you?" said Cecilia.

Jo turned to look at the other riders. They were all standing quite still. Some were shaking their heads as if to clear them. Others were frowning in concentration. Mr. Angelo was standing alone nearby. He was staring at the carousel, looking puzzled. Then, as she watched, he shrugged, grinned, looked at his watch, and strolled away toward Marley Street. But the expression of hope that had warmed his face remained. He walked back to his shop and the hard work ahead with a spring in his step.

Mr. Milligan was looking hard at his little bank on the corner, biting his lip. He tapped his fingers on his forehead and shook his head slightly. Then he straightened his shoulders, hitched at his belt, and walked on with rather a jaunty air.

The man in the brown trousers stood by the sidewalk. He stroked his chin, a furrow between his eyebrows. Then he, too, shrugged. He pushed his hand deep into his pocket and pulled out a handkerchief. Some pieces of yellow paper fell to the ground, with a chewing-gum wrapper and a few old bus tickets. He kicked at them idly with his foot but made no effort to pick them up. He blew his nose, stuffed the handkerchief back in his pocket, then crossed the road without looking back.

The wind gathered up the litter he had dropped and gently tumbled it away with the leaves.

Jo looked back at the carousel. It stood there glimmering in the morning sun. Leaning against the brass poles were three figures—an old man, an old woman, and between them a tall, red-headed boy. They were laughing together as if they shared some private joke. Jo stared. There was something familiar about that boy. . . . Something . . .

"Look, Jo, I'm going! I'll see you on Monday," snapped Cecilia.

"Okay," said Jo absently. Cecilia gave a snort of disgust and flounced away. Jo stood for a moment, thinking. The red-headed boy on the carousel lifted his arm—in greeting or farewell. She waved back and, smiling, turned away for home.

16

"I Just Have This Feeling . . ."

Jo walked down Marley Street, feeling the swirl of leaves around her feet. Soon the trees would be quite bare, and then, after a little while, the green leaves would shoot and unfold from the dry, clattering branches, and the whole cycle would start again. She felt a lightness of heart. Every year, as the new leaves appeared, the trees grew a little taller. They changed, and they grew—but they were still the same trees. Funny, she'd never thought about it in quite that way before.

She crossed Lily Street and remembered walking home the day before, feeling miserable and unsettled. For some reason that seemed a long time ago, as if a lot had happened since. And now she felt quite different, as though she'd solved something in her own mind.

But nothing had happened, had it? She stopped and wrinkled her forehead. Something flickered at the edge of her mind. Was it something she'd forgotten?

"Jo!"

Jo looked up and saw her mother strolling up the street toward her.

"I thought I might meet you. I heard there was a merry-go-round up at the shops. Did you and Cecilia have a ride?"

"Yes . . . I think we did—I mean, we did."

"Good. Listen, Jo, I've got something to tell you."

Jo looked into her mother's face—at the tumbled black hair, the gentle dark eyes, the pointed chin.

"We decided last night it was time to tell you. We've been waiting till we knew it was absolutely sure before we told you, because we thought—Well—"

"What is it, Mum?" Yet somehow Jo knew.

"Well—we're going to . . ."

"We're going to have a *baby!* Mum! That's it, isn't it? I know it is!"

"Jo!" Her mother laughed. "How on earth did you . . . ?"

Then she put her hand on Jo's arm. "You don't mind, do you, Jo?" she said softly.

Jo looked at her. "All my friends would love their mums to have a baby. Cecilia'll be really envious."

"But you're not all your friends. And . . . you're not crazy about changes. I know you'd feel you *had* to say you were happy. But are you really, Jo?"

Jo thought. She thought of moving out of the only house she knew, into a strange one. She thought of a new baby demanding all sorts of changes to their lives, and a big share of her parents' attention. She thought of having to be the grown-up one, the big sister instead of the baby.

And then, with a sudden, warm rush, another set of thoughts flooded her mind. Pictures and feelings as strong as memories . . . small, grubby fingers clutching at her hand, a trusting face looking up at her with dark brown eyes, a rough black head leaning heavily on her arm. And a voice. *Won't I see you anymore?* Her eyes filled with tears. It was so real! Where . . . ?

"Jo, darling, don't cry."

"I'm very happy, Mum. I'll love him. I'll love having him."

Her mother's face broke into a relieved, happy smile. "Oh, Jo," she said. "We don't know if it's a boy or a girl yet."

"Oh, no . . . of course we don't." Jo was bewildered for a moment. "I just have this feeling . . ."

"Well, you might be right. I've got no feeling this time. But I just *knew* you were going to be a little girl. It's funny, though. . . . I always somehow pictured you as the age you are now. It was as though I'd seen you, grown up, before you were even born. Isn't that strange?"

"Yes," said Jo, and again some idea danced at the fringes of her mind.

They turned in at the familiar gate.

"Jo," said Helen cautiously, "Mike and I are going to look at some houses this afternoon. Two on Telford Avenue, and one on Singer Street. Would you like to come with us?"

"Of *course* I would. I want to help choose! It'll be my house too."

"Yes, it will!" Helen put her hands on Jo's shoulders. "Jo, you take my breath away. You seem to have grown up overnight. And you're getting so tall. That reminds me. . . ." She put the key in the lock, and Podge's claws began clattering on the floor of the hall. "In the new house we'll have more room. Room for a piano, if you'd like to learn. It's a bit late, but you've always said . . ."

97

Podge was barking now and leaping against the door. Michael was shouting at her to be quiet, Helen was still talking, her usually pale face glowing with hopes and plans, and the wind blew the leaves, clattering, down Marley Street. But Jo heard none of this. For again her ears were filled with music.

17

Kids' Stuff?

They were in the kitchen having morning tea when the doorbell rang.

"Oh, that'll be Simon," said Helen. "I asked him in for a cup. He looked so down this morning."

"Can we tell him, Mum?" asked Jo excitedly.

Her parents exchanged glances. "Why not?" said Michael. "He's one of the family, really, isn't he?"

But when Simon shuffled into the kitchen, smiling at them uncertainly, it was obvious that this wasn't the time for breaking the good news. He looked worn out and miserable, and somehow, Jo thought, defeated. Her heart ached for him as he sat down carefully at the table, coughing softly. His thin shoulders in the old gray cardigan were rounded and bent, and his hands were unsteady as he took the cup of tea Michael put down in front of him. Jo had known him all her life, and for the first time he looked old to her.

She shook her head. She was sure she had something she meant to tell him. Something—something—not about the baby, but something else that he'd find really interesting, that would cheer him up. But for the life of her she couldn't remember what it was.

"How was it then, little Yo?" asked Simon.

"What?" Jo looked at him, confused.

"The merry-go-round. The music we heard. I saw your friend coming back home earlier."

"Oh, it was okay," said Jo. I guess, she thought. I don't seem to remember much about it.

"I wish I'd been able to get up to see it with you," said Simon. He shook his head. "Not that it matters. Silly, really. Kids' stuff . . . Like the inventing—wanting to be an inventor, of all things. Kids' stuff. Dreams. Ivy Pickering's right. Time I grew up, isn't it? And faced up to the failure I am."

"You're not a failure!" Jo protested. "It's not silly. Your safety lock really works. Your plug works. Your . . ."

Simon sighed and smiled sadly. "Never caught on, though, did they?" he said. "Not one of them. No one would lend me the money to get them produced and into the shops." He sighed again. "Just one big success, that was all I needed," he said. "One thing that caught on."

"It'll happen, Simon," said Michael.

"Yes, Simon, it'll happen," echoed Helen's soft voice. "Give it time."

"Time's run out, it seems, Helen," said Simon quietly. "This morning—just now, in fact, I've been told I have to leave my flat next month. They're throwing me out. After fifteen years. I'm behind with the rent, as it happens. And Ivy Pickering has complained . . ."

"Oh, no!" Helen put her hand on his arm, but he shook his head and smiled.

"Let's not talk about it, Helen dear. I'd really

100

rather not. Oh—I forgot . . ." From a plastic bag under his chair he pulled out a bunch of green leaves wrapped in newspaper. "Some fresh mint and parsley, Helen. And Yo—another little invention for you. I made it while I was laid up. You might have some fun with it. Or just put it with your collection of Simon Crisp originals, eh?" He laughed bitterly. "They're all originals, aren't they? Never been a second one of any of them. Well . . ."

Jo wandered away from the table, clutching Simon's gift. She stood looking out the window, and began idly to play with it.

"No, no," she heard her old friend say. "It's all over. I'm going to pull myself together now and be sensible. No more wasting money on patents and expensive bits and pieces to make into things no one wants to buy."

Jo looked down at what she was doing. Like all Simon's inventions, this one was really quite interesting. She began experimenting with it.

"Just give it one more try," said Helen persuasively. "Go and see old Milligan, up at the bank we go to, on the corner. He's giving us a loan for the new house. Take up a couple of your things and show him, Simon. He might give you a little loan, to tide you over."

"He's a bit of a stick-in-the-mud, Helen," said Michael dubiously. "Never been known to take a chance in his life. He might think Simon's, or anyone's, inventions were a bit risky to put the bank's money into, and . . ." His voice trailed away. He was watching Jo. He nudged Helen, and together they stared at their daughter and the object that made patterns in the air above her feet.

"Quite right," said Simon. He looked at his hands. "Don't worry about it—please don't. It's my problem. I've got nothing new to show him anyway. Nothing he'd be interested in."

Jo spoke, almost to herself, and without taking her eyes off her play. "What about this?" she murmured. "Simon, what about this?"

"That's just a toy, Yody." Simon smiled at her gently. "A man like Mr. Milligan would never be interested in—"

"Simon—I wouldn't be too sure about that," said Michael slowly. "That thing's not bad at all. How did you do it?"

"He *would*. He *would* be interested. I can feel it. I *know!*" Jo spun around to face them. "Simon! You said you needed something that would catch on, didn't you? Get to be a craze? This is it! I know it is! And Mr. Milligan will see it too. Simon, please try it. Go on!"

In Simon's pale blue eyes, behind the gold-rimmed glasses, a small ray of hope dawned. He watched his creation as it spun and danced in the air at the bidding of Jo's fingers.

"You really think so, Yo?" he said, shaking his head.

"She's very sure, Simon. I'd listen to her if I were you," said Helen. "She's running hot with these 'feelings' today, and she's been right on so far. Let me drive you up to the bank on Monday morning. Milligan could lend you a bit. Could even recommend to his head office that you get a real development loan. It is . . . it is a marvelous thing, Simon. I can't take my eyes off it."

"I'll say," said Michael. "Look at it go!"

Simon was grinning broadly now. He ran a trembling finger around the inside of his collar and pulled at it as if it were too tight. "It's, I think, the string that is the masterstroke," he said proudly. "Catches the light, you see." Suddenly he pulled off his glasses and thumped the table with his other hand.

"I'll try it!" he said. "I'll do it. I'll see Milligan on Monday. He may want to take a chance, just this once." He rubbed his hands. His eyes were alight with energy and hope. He looked like his old self again.

"Oh, good for you, Simon," said Helen. "Look— will you look at that thing! Jo—you've caught on to it so fast!"

Jo laughed and ran out into the courtyard to give herself more room. She felt like shouting aloud. She felt like holding her arms out and hugging the whole world.

"It needs a good name," Simon called to her, nodding violently and chewing the arm of his glasses. "A catchy name is very important."

"You'll think of something," yelled Jo. "You always do. Oh, you wait. In a few years every second kid'll have one of these. I can see it, like a picture. Millions of them—everywhere. And I've got number one! The original!"

"A catchy name," murmured Simon. "Now . . . ah . . . Oh, I've got it! I've got it! Little Yo, are you listening? Now, how about . . ."

Jo yelled with delight. She twirled the silver string, and the original, the very first of five million Yo-Balls, went spinning, once again, into the sun.